What I Know

I Cannot Say

All That Lies Beneath

Dai Smith

Betrayers

Soixante Huitards, all

"Thirty three minutes straight through to the city," he'd said. "Thirty three minutes of commuter hell in the week," he'd added. "No time at all, though, on a Sunday or a Holiday, with empty seats and no need to stand either part or all of the way. She'll sleep it off," he was sure of it. "Take a window seat, enjoy the view, let her head rest on your shoulder. Be a mensch!" he urged. He told him he was one lucky son-of-a-gun, for a Welsh guy that is, as he helped to push her up the steep metal steps into the railroad car. "You'll be there in no time, kiddo," he called out as he stepped back down. Mamaroneck to Manhattan, a slider from Westchester County to New York City. Downhill all the way to the Big Apple. Then he said, his height allowing him almost to speak into the half opened window of the carriage, and he snapped his words out this time, that "Thirty three was a good number, the age Christ was when those bastards got him." "Don't forget the rule of numbers," he shouted as the train began to shudder. He had earlier expanded on the theme. Sixty minutes to the hour sounds a lot, perhaps, but minutes were all we really had to hold fast to, moments not processes, and by no means could anything as big as a single year or as impossible as a decade be grasped in retrospect. Instants of for instance will be all that will be left inside you to recall memory. " So goodbye," he said.

The dirty ochre train ground its way along the sunken platform where he still stood waving. The overhead neon tubes of the station picked him out, shape and size only now, in the fading light of the early winter. He waved rather alarmingly. He flapped at the air in front of him with his huge open palmed hands. It looked like a warning, this jerky, ill-coordinated wave. He was shouting some last words at

1

the departing train. The train clattered past some sidings. It left the town behind. The last of the day's sun dropped in the west before the train. Outside, it had become dark where they had been. Inside, the railway car glimmered a dim orange. On the train their profiles were reflected in an unwashed window. He moved slightly, so as not to disturb her, so that he could look into his own full face, front on. This was all in less than a minute amongst the recent hours which had passed. A moment that won't ever be discarded, he thought. Or so he said to himself, in echo of his late host, at that moment of parting.

* * * * *

When they had set out from Grand Central Station at noon, winter sunshine had funnelled down into the city streets and splintered itself on the tall glass and metal buildings in the avenues. The sun darted and sparkled over and through the iron fretwork of the trestle bridges by which they left the city – and as the train went north the sun scratched diamond points on the row upon row of windows glinting from the high rise project housing in Harlem. They sat closely together on the train and he felt her pressing into him in her need to be calm and contain the anticipation which had built and built inside her for days. The train rattled along its elevated track until the city was reduced in its lee to shining battlements. And then the turquoise blue waters of the Hudson flanked it on its left-hand side, and on out into the country and to their destination in fabled Westchester County. The Mamaroneck home of Saul Kellerman. It was Thanksgiving Day, 24th November 1966.

Every year the foreign students at International House on Riverside Drive and 125th street were assigned by lot random invitations to the American homes of IH supporters for the Thanksgiving Holiday, when life in the New World was ritually celebrated with a dose of gratitude and excess. He'd drawn the Kellerman invite. He hadn't really thought to accept it until he told her. Then the quivering and the Omigods had begun as she, in turn, told him who Kellerman was. To meet him in the flesh, so to speak, for her she said, would be too, too amazing. He had to go. He could take a friend. He must, please, please, take her. He could see at once that it would do him no harm, the opposite in fact, in their on-going relationship. They had slept together already so there was no gain for him there beyond a further assurance. He felt somewhat uneasy thinking in that way but there it was, that was the way it was, and he wanted to keep hold of her, intimately, for a while yet. At least until he went home.

He met her at a party in the Village. She'd been lolling on an armchair, her right bare arm outstretched, a slow-burning cigarette, or was it a joint maybe, dangling between two fingers of her left. She was talking to two men stood over her. She was, he discovered, inclined to talk. Her skirt rose up above her long outstretched legs. Yellow-stockinged legs. And when she stood up, later, he saw that she was a half-head taller than him, and by no means what his dwt of a mother would have called petite. Nor was she, in conventional eyes, pretty. But in that less conventional decade and unconventional place she was, as they said, a striking-looking girl. An explosion of tawny-blonde hair framed her square jawed face, and kohl-lined eyes drew you in past their black circle to the glitter of her blue eyes which seemed to smile at you even before she actually smiled. She had smiled at him, indeed, the moment he spoke. His accent intrigued them all. What was it, they asked. For him, that of Mary Ellen Robinson from Baton Rouge, Louisiana was just as exotic, intriguingly so. She was on a graduate course in Jurisprudence at Columbia University. New York City, added as a clincher. He was, she told him, the first boy from England she'd ever met. And even after he'd explained that he came from Wales she would ask him about England.

After six months in New York he'd made it all easier by just saying, "This is Burr-naard Jenkins. And you are?" That way he didn't need

3

to correct their pronunciation, as if they were in the wrong ,and the mode of introduction, open and enquiring in the American manner, was one he'd quickly learned to adopt. He'd tell them he was on a graduate fellowship to work on particle physics, neutrons, after his first, stellar degree at Manchester. The name of that northern English city would usually lead on to the Beatles and a few helpful pointers from him, especially if his questioners were female, as to the proximity of Liverpool to Manchester. Special knowledge was implied. Places he really knew about, the stuff about Wales, was a harder sell since neither the name of the place nor the country's existence registered with those Americans, of either sex, he might meet in seminars, in bars, in parties. He allowed himself to be from England. And his name was indeed Burr-naard. And he now had a further advantage, at least so far as Mary Ellen Robinson was concerned: a date with Saul Kellerman, which, naturally, in the light of her excitement, he'd accepted.

Mary Ellen, ever since he'd given her the good news, could not stop fluttering at the prospect. She informed him, over and over, of the stature of the man they were to meet on Thanksgiving. And in his own home. Omigod she couldn't believe it, she said.

"Look at me, Burr-naard, I'm pinching myself," she said. "The Saul Kellerman. Wow," she said. "Can you believe it?" she asked. He said he could. "But, listen," she said, sitting up in bed with him, "do you know? You do, don't you? He's the most outstanding Civil Rights lawyer of the day. Of his generation. In America, all of America," she said.

He told her that he guessed he'd got it by now. That didn't stop her reeling off the cases Kellerman had fought and won. Against all the odds. Cases that were history already. Legislation in the making, case law, triumphs of forensic argument and moral courage. He'd caused moral outrage in her native South by defending freedom-riders and civil disobedience activists, whether black or white. Kellerman was fearless. A reputation made in the 1950s as an advocate of the rights of Labor and Union organisation was put to one side, along with lucrative remuneration, for Kellerman had been radicalised by the injustice being suffered by black Americans who were daring to assert their rights. He was not the only good liberal legal practitioner to re-act like that but he was alone in the scope and intent of his advocacy. He sloughed off his middle age and his respectability. Mary Ellen was not sure what most offended people like her parents, whether it was what he was doing or how he was doing it. The 'what' had already begun to gather to include anti-war dissidents and direct-action protesters, and the 'how' had started to become displays of histrionics, in court after court, aping the outrageous otherness of his pro-bono clients. When judges called for self-control and demanded respect he accused them of acts of repression. When he was ejected from courts and barred from cases he was fighting, he compared the appointed judges to the Nazis he'd fought in Normandy, and in the Ardennes at the Battle of the Bulge. If a particular judge was a Jew, Kellerman made it personal between 'two nice Jewish boys like you and me', and asked if his friends had died in those snow-filled forests in 1944 in vain. For what? For nothing? Or for the Freedom they thought they were defending against repression.

Mary Ellen had a file of newspaper cuttings of his cases, and grainy newsprint photographs. She had shown them to Burr-naard. This one of Kellerman being thrown out of a courthouse in Georgia by police marshals. This one of Kellerman, without coat or neck-tie, harangueing a crowd of supporters the very next day on the steps of the same courtroom. Another of Kellerman under arrest in a state trooper's car in Oxford, Mississippi. And Kellerman pushed to the ground. Kellerman interviewed. Kellerman profiled. Kellerman denounced on the Op Ed pages of heavyweight newspapers. Kellerman lionised in campus mimeographs. Kellerman speaking at student anti-war rallies across the USA. Kellerman urged to run for political office. Kellerman everywhere, using the Press as a platform, even as it denigrated him. Kellerman the most vital force against the legal establishment from within its ranks since Clarence Darrow in the 1920s. Kellerman was a sensation. Kellerman was a phenomenon. Kellerman was her Hero and he was waiting for them at the railroad station in Mamaroneck, Westchester. Omigod.

Whatever prospect of self-fulfilment was in Mary Ellen's mind as the suburban train pulled into the station, was not matched by Bernard. Here, in 1966, in America he was already fulfilled. He was, daily, astounded that he was there at all. A life to that point only pricked out, amidst the normal flatness of his existence, by the American jag of disturbance, which came from a distance and acted across his senses with music and movies and perhaps promises of power to take what you wanted when you wanted it, had somehow been transported into the whole of his life ,and day by day. Americans of his generation did not seem to stop to savour this. He did, astonished not by what might happen, in any specific way, to him next but by what, in general, was making him float where once he had trudged. He was not yet twenty-two.

He was, for the first time in his entire post-war life, made buoyant by the depth of sensation which he felt day by day, and it was enough to keep him poised on the verge of a grateful wonder for the New World, and all its works. Simple stuff, really. Like an Idaho baked potato, as big as a small rock, its mottled brown papery skin slashed open so that its fluffy white insides would be slathered yellow with dollops of butter. He would wait in line at the cafeteria to have a T-bone steak, something he'd never seen before, grilled and plonked onto his plate to match the baked potato in its size and desirability. All for $1.25. Or breathing in the city's compound heat in Columbus Circle at midnight,with traffic still in an endless flow all around him, and drinking an Orange Julius. The drink such an unlikely concoction of juice and milk and sugar and vanilla flavouring, a supreme if peculiar blend of the tart and the sweet, and loved by New Yorkers since the 1920s as proclaimed by the strapline above the Juice Bar. He believed it, and he joined the line of addicts. Its syrupy tanginess chilled cold in a paper cup tasted a world away from the tepid, watery orange juice in half-pint glass bottles from his welfare childhood. As far away as the ersatz coffee of his undergraduate days compared to the rich, brown succulence of American coffee and the endless, free re-fills offered and drunk along with iced water whilst perched at a Diner's counter on a white leather-seated high stool. The unfriendliness of this scary city exhilarated him. It made no demands. It let you be. It promised nothing. It suggested everything. Nothing about it from first light to electric night was insipid. Nothing was lukewarm. Nothing was quite how it seemed. Nowhere was less like home where nooks and crannies of people and memory could always offer the comfort of relapse. Bernard loved to wear the mask which the city had given him.

* * * * *

Now, the movie in which he was so unexpectedly starring provided a new GV for his POV. From the train window, opening up its vista on the wealth of the citizens who had fled the city for up-state living of style and substance, he surveyed the America that thought it was Camelot. No location, she'd told him, was more stylish or required more substantial income than Mamaroneck in Westchester County. On this sunny day, in the crisp air, the French -blue and antique- white clapboard colonial houses played their part on his film set. So, too, did the tail-finned pastel coloured Chryslers and the sleeker Buicks, metallic bronze and boat-like in dimension, parked haphazardly but carefully in the lot by the station. Telephone wires criss-crossed overhead from ranks of wooden poles and gave the whole picture the small-town feel of the earlier America which this America still loved to memorialise in sentiment and song. The cast had assembled, on the train and those waiting for it on the platform: women in long top-coats, holding the hands of children in lumber jackets and jeans; men in light, fawn and belted raincoats, but hatless, or with windcheaters zipped up over plaid shirts. Greetings. Kisses. Modulated shouts. The only black faces were those in attendance on the train or on the platform as station porters. They stood out, but only if they were noticed, and no-one noticed. Bernard and Mary Ellen were more conspicuous, being young and students, he in a faded pink button-down shirt he'd bought in the university Co-op and wore without a tie over his old university blazer to make him feel himself to be, from his new Levis to his new Penny Loafers, an all-American American, albeit one considerably shorter than the norm; and she, holding his hand, her thickly-tressed hair falling loose and long over a man's white shirt and a raspberry-red cardigan, with her long yellow-stockinged legs on show beneath a dark grey, almost mini-skirt. She had chosen flat shoes to stay as decently level as she could with her exotic Englishman from Wales. They, too, attracted no real attention, unless you were looking out for them. And then, right in front of them was Kellerman himself, so that Mary Ellen stopped abruptly and Bernard Jenkins nearly stumbled into her.

He stood before them, blocking their path and that of any others who might be coming behind them, and he opened his arms high and wide as if he were a windmill ready for motion. His splayed arms looked as if they had extensions at the elbow so that his forearms seemed longer than was proportionate and his hands, black wiry hair curling wildly over their backs and their knuckles, were as broad as a longshoreman's and as long-fingered as those of a classical pianist. He was also plainly huge. Not fleshy anywhere but over-sized everywhere. His head. His round, black eyes in deep-set bony sockets. His chest which expanded away from his shoulders which were themselves as wide as a bedroom's tallboy. Nor did he fit his three piece, green tweed suit which sat on him as if it had been pre-shrunk on his frame.

Nothing about him was congruent, from his black and scuffed sneakers to his white T-shirt underneath an open-necked, navy blue poplin shirt. Kellerman was six feet four but somehow seemed even taller since above the bald expanse of his head, but coming from the sides, was a riot, a tangle, an electrified bush of grey and black hair which gave him an unlikely halo. Hair sprouted from inside the top of his T-shirt. Hair bristled from the black recesses at the tip of his prow of a nose and stuck out like needles where he had shaved. Hair cascaded in hirsute rillettes from his shaggy eyebrows and shaded his eyes. His arms whirled up and around, and unexpectedly on the downward movement clamped Mary Ellen close to him whilst somehow managing to flip Bernard into their embrace as they did. When he spoke it was in a deep growling tone.

"Hi'y'a kids. How you doing? Trip okay? Here you are, then. I'm Saul Kellerman by the way. Car's over here , Okay?"

They were propelled rather than guided by this bear of a man who had grabbed them and taken them on, to the parking bays beyond the platform, and thrust them into the back seat of a Ford Sedan. The car was old, dented in places and less shiny than the gleaming newer models parked around it. Kellerman's car reeked with the stale fug of cigarette smoke and the leather-panelled seats were sticky with the discarded wrappers of chocolate Hershey bars and packets of Lifesavers whose mintiness had not lingered. Kellerman wheeled his car out of its bay with no regard for the other vehicles politely jockeying their way past one another. He accelerated immediately with the confidence of a driver born to crash, sometime soon, or indeed again.

"It isn't far," he had told them, whilst going through an overhanging red light and swerving off Main Street. "Maybe ten, fifteen minutes say," he had said and, "See if we can make it quicker, beat the numbers, must need a shot by now," and he'd grinned in the driver's mirror at his passengers. Apart from a few gulped hellos, neither Mary Ellen nor Bernard, had spoken. She was gripping Bernard's hand, not in fright at Kellerman's fast and erratic driving, but still a-quiver with the delight of all that was happening to her. Once out of town, the white sedan skidded down intersecting blacktop roads until, near the ocean, it began to pass small copses with houses half-hidden by the closely planted trees. They were each slightly different, these detached houses, though all were fairly recent, modern split-level dwellings aproned by driveways, and fronting the lawns and woodland which sloped gently to the shore at their rear.

"Twelve minutes exact," he said triumphantly and tapped a watch that could have doubled for a chronometer on a navy vessel. He slid the battered sedan onto one such driveway in front of one such house, and fiercely wrenched up the car's brake. He jumped out, opened the back passenger doors and then slammed them shut just as sharply, so that Mary Ellen and Bernard had to skip to one side. Kellerman made a wide circle with his arms again, and said, "Okay then. Home fuckin' sweet home, kids. Welcome to Chez Kellerman. Come on in, come on in," and he strode a pace or two in front of his guests into his house.

Bernard Jenkins had never previously been inside, or indeed outside, an open plan house. At home the concept of a knock-through from front room to back room or kitchen was in its infancy in terraced houses entered by the corridor of a hall, or passageway as his parents would say. In the newest of New Worlds he paused at the edge of a house-wide glass wall which led into an atrium filled with plants, their broad green leaves and palpitating fronds set to one side of a stone path laid over a channel of murmuring water, and which led on after a few yards to more sliding glass doors. Then through them into a floor to ceiling space which ran all the way to the back of the house where a final set of glass doors revealed an outside patio with low field-stone walls and some steps down to a shaved lawn stretching into a distant prospect of deciduous trees, some still gaudy with colour in their defiantly late fall glad rags.

Once inside the house, Bernard took in the rooms-within-rooms, each effortlessly interlocked seamlessly without any separating walls. There were sitting areas, two of them, with brown leather club chairs around a low walnut table in one, and in the other, a larger space, there was a more elaborate set of sofas and chairs in a block buttercup-yellow fabric, and occasional glass-topped, coffee tables with burnished steel tubular legs set on bright Navajo zig-zag rugs. In the far right-hand corner were packed book shelves. Spiralling oak-stepped stairs rose to a wrap-around gallery with doors leading off its corridor into bedroom spaces under the roof. On the left-hand side, beyond the living spaces and behind a maple-wood dividing counter, were high-backed dining chairs and a long rectangular cherry-wood table. The kitchen area, at the very back of the whole space, had a wood and marble topped stand-alone unit inset with electric hobs, two ceramic sinks, chopping boards and hooks to hold a battery of culinary instruments. Someone, somehow, had made it all come together as a whole.

Sat on the buttercup- yellow couch, a thick glass tumbler of ice and liquor in her hand, was an unsmiling, dark-haired woman whom Kellerman airily introduced by another expansive wave of his hand.

"Oh, yeah. Kids. Meet the wife. Mrs Kellerman. The First. The Last. And Only. Rachie, meet the kids."

Rachel Kellerman stood. She put her drink down onto a glass table with a clunk as it slipped slightly from her grasp. "Hi, I'm Rachel. He hasn't asked you your names yet, has he? So, 'kids', welcome and may I ask your names."

Saul Kellerman had moved on to a drinks cabinet with a drop-down shelf. He was unabashed. He was unrestrained. He shouted across the room.

"Kids! Whaddya'l take? Bourbon, ok? Wild Turkey or Jack's? Or a beer if you like. Miller or Schlitz, I think. There's wine with the food, I guess. I hope!"

Rachel Kellerman, in her turn, ignored her husband. The First. The Last. The Only. She took a couple of steps across a waxed pine floor towards the 'kids' and extended her hand. First, to Mary Ellen who shook it, too hard, and gulped.

"I'm Mary Ellen, Mrs Kellerman. Mary Ellen Robinson, that is." Then the hand, a single gold band on her third finger, was in Bernard's and rested there a little longer. "So you must be the English guy."

Bernard nodded. Her hand remained in his, soft and quite still. Rachel Kellerman was not as tall as Mary Ellen but, in her kitten heeled leopard-print shoes, a little taller than Bernard who looked up into the appraisal of her opaque brown eyes. The gold wedding ring was the only jewellery she wore. Bernard could feel its smooth, rounded bump nestling in his hand. She was without make-up except for a vivid scarlet lipstick. She was dressed with an elegance accentuated by its casualness: dark-grey slacks with the new permanent crease and a see-through long-sleeved black chiffon blouse with small stand-out lime green polka dots. Bernard knew he was staring. Bernard could not stop staring. The forty-something Rachel Kellerman tilted her head and gave him an inquisitive smile.

"This is Burr-naard Jenkins," he stuttered. She took her hand away at last. She said, "And what will you have to drink, Burr-naaard?"

"I'll, uh, have, uh, Wild Turkey, please," he said, and added, as if he'd always had it that way. "On the rocks, please."

Rachel glanced at Mary Ellen who said she'd have the same. Rachel half-turned to her husband who'd already busied himself fixing a stiff Jack Daniels straight, with water back, for himself. His wife told him, "Mary Ellen will have a Wild Turkey, and so will Burrn-aard from England. Both with ice, honey." Saul Kellerman reached out to pluck a different bottle from the shelves of bottles to his front. He chunked ice cubes out of a stainless steel tray and clunked them into two glasses. He poured the bourbon whisky onto the ice without measuring it. He carried the drinks over to the 'kids' and handed them one each. He retrieved his own glass and joined the now seated company where his guests were on the sofa which Rachel had indicated, and herself back on her chosen chair. She lit an untipped cigarette and blew smoke her husband's way. Wispy twists of smoke drifted through his wild hair and on into the beams of sunlight with which his halo was backlit. He stood, he hovered, above the 'kids'. He made a puzzled move, with a downturned jut of his lip.

"Burrn-aard," he said. "That's American, kid. You cannot, be really called Burrn-aard, can you? What's your real name, buddy?"

"Well" said Bernard Jenkins to the prosecuting counsel, "Well, Mr Kellerman. I do, you see, call myself that now. For convenience sake, I mean. Here, I call myself, Burr-naard. Here in America, I mean. People, uh, seem to understand that pronunciation, without explanation."

"People are dumb," said Saul Kellerman. "I'll call you Bernard, and you can call me Saul, eh kid?"

His wife blew anther cloud of cigarette smoke at him. "And you, kid," he said to Mary Ellen. "Any trouble with your name?"

"No, Mr Kellerman. No. I'm just plain Mary Ellen Robinson".

Kellerman opened up his arms, pleading his case before any so assembled. He leaned over her as if he might scoop her up into them, as predator or prosecutor, or both at once.

"Plain, you're not, sister," he said "Don't ever call yourself plain. We're all beautiful. In and for ourselves, aren't we Rachie?" he asked his wife in mock appeal.

Rachel Kellerman slurped a large mouthful of bourbon. She kept her glass in her hand. She did not reply. Her husband, his eyes never leaving Mary Ellen's up-turned face, said, in a softer tone of enquiry.

"Where y'all from, then, Mary Ellen? The South, I can tell. I'm guessing the Deep South, I'd guess, Mississippi. Good Ole Mississippi. Though Alabama'd be worse!"

"I'm from Baton Rouge. The state capital of Louisiana," Mary Ellen rapped out.

"Baton Rouge, huh? Say, that's not so bad. Not sure about the bayou-dwellers of that ridiculously called Pelican State of yours, but you got some brains left in Baton Rouge, for sure. And some bright sparks in New Orleans too – Noo Orlins, pardon me. I've even got a soft spot in me, old Leftie as I was, for that wild man from the Thirties, that you once had there. At least he had a social conscience did Governor Huey P. Long, huh?". Saul Kellerman swivelled apologetically towards Bernard. "Oh, excuse me, Bernard. American history, and all that. You ever hear of The Kingfish, Bernard?"

"Oh come on Saul" said his wife. "It's Thanksgiving. A holiday. No lectures today, puh-lease!"

"Thanksgiving for some, for sure" went on Kellerman, no diversions allowed to re-direct him once in full-flow. "Thanksgiving, for sure. I know. But for what? For why? And since us folks giving the thanks are New York Jews we can afford to share a little intellectual meatiness with our Columbia graduate students, can't we kids? And besides the Kingfish is very relevant to Thanksgiving."

Rachel Kellerman stubbed out the cigarette in a mottled green onyx ashtray. She stood up. She said, looking at her husband, that it was time to freshen her glass. Bernard loved the phrase. It spoke to him of new beginnings, new continuities, re-calibrated narratives. Not of old stories, backstories, she might have heard before. Over and over. Kellerman called out to her retreating, arched back, to remember not to forget the troops.

"Share the wealth, baby," he said, "just like 'ole Kingfish told us, every man's a king, huh?" He reached across Bernard and patted Mary Ellen's hand. She jumped, startled, pleased.

"Bernard," said Saul Kellerman, "this young lady, from Loo-ees-ee-ana, is neglecting your education if she fails to inform you of her state's greatest, most deplorable, politician of this century. The Kingfish.

Governor Huey Long." Saul Kellerman paused. He assumed his adversarial pose. "You do know about him, don't you, kid?" he asked. "And I'm guessing, too, that even now, what thirty one years near enough to the day, your family, your folks in Baton Rouge, are not exactly, strictly, enamoured of that rascal, are they?"

Mary Ellen recognised the question to be a statement. She was not sure if it entailed an answer. In any case, Saul Kellerman did not wait for one. He half-turned to Bernard as his wife brought a tray of fresh whiskies for them, and a refreshed one for herself. Kellerman took a swallow and wiped his expansive mouth with the back of his left hand.

"In the thirties, Bernard, America was in the shit. I mean deep-shit. No, I'll re-phrase that. Capitalism was our sewer and it was drowning Americans in its shit. And in the sewer were the rats. The rich. The big corporations. Swimming in the sewer. Heads above all the little guys. All washed up. Unemployment in double digits across the nation. Poverty. Dirt poverty. Depression. The Great Depression. And in Louisiana, worse than that, on top of all that, decades of subservience. A feudal system, Bernard, in twentieth-century America. Dirt-poor tenant farmers. White. Sharecroppers. Black. Illiteracy. Non-voter registration. Shit schools. Shit roads. Shit jobs. Or no jobs. And a cabal of southern gentlemen sucking on their mint-juleps, avoiding tax revenue on their oil fields and riding, high and mighty, roughshod over a whole state. The nineteen thirties? Shit. Louisiana was still in the eighteen thirties! Then Huey P. Long. The 'P' stands for Pierce by the way. Huey P Long stormed in, on a wave of indignation, to become Governor in 1928. The Kingfish. No one wears a crown, said the king. This king soaked the rich. This king built roads. This king built bridges. This king gave the rural and the urban poor a chance, in unity. This king built hospitals. With tax-raised revenue. This king built schools. This king built state capital buildings in your Baton Rouge, Mary Ellen. They tried to stop him. So he beat them up, he humiliated them, he scorned them. He built up the state militia, the police, a personal cohort of body guards. In America. If he was hated, and he was, so he was loved, and he was. They tried to stop him, any way they could Bernard. He was unstoppable."

Saul Kellerman finished his drink. Rachel Kellerman had given up trying to stop him. Her husband was unstoppable.

"What happened is" he said, "that the Governor now ran for Senator. And won again. In Washington he was, as Roosevelt's so-called New Deal crept along,way to the left of that patrician phoney and, maybe, just maybe, setting to run for President himself, in 1936 or 1940, on a Share the Wealth ticket. Who knows, he could've won. If he had I wouldn't have been trailing my GI Jewish butt around Europe."

"Unstoppable. Until they stopped him. Stopped him dead. In his tracks. Shot him. Killed Huey. Assassinated the Kingfish. Some well-connected patsy called Carl Weiss put a bullet in the Governor's stomach in the marble halls of the Baton Rouge State Capitol building. In 1935. Huey Long was forty two years old. Convenient, for some, huh, Bernard?"

Mary Ellen flushed at the base of her throat as if she had, personally, done something reprehensible. She could see her father, a Baton Rouge medical practitioner, slapping their dining table with glee every time he recalled, and it was often enough when she was growing up, where he was the day that evil man was shot dead. Mary Ellen loved her daddy. Mary Ellen said that she was sure there were good things to say about Huey Long but that, surely, he was also very corrupt, lined his own pockets. Made people he'd put on the public pay roll, pay him back in percentages. Had his thugs beat up his respectable opponents. That the Long family became a dynasty, too, and erected a huge statue to their founding figure outside the State Capitol building. That he stole from people's legitimate, inherited wealth, making him, some thought she had said, no better than a communist. Mary Ellen then said that she could see maybe older people back home, not her generation, might not see things quite the way Mr Kellerman had put it.

Saul Kellerman sat back in his armchair. He smiled at Mary Ellen and nodded. "You're right about that, kiddo. But, you know, he wasn't a Commie. And he wasn't, despite Rooseveltian slurs in the Press ,any kind of a Fascist. He was much more dangerous than that. He was American through-and-through. A good old, old fashioned Southern Populist, brought bang-up-to-date. That's what he was. Oh, unscrupulous. Unworthy. Undignified. Yes. A rabble-rouser. Yes. A demagogue. Yes. And, just maybe, in a corrupt world, he was corruptible enough to be a game-changer. All from, Lou-ee-zee-anna, like your girl friend Mary Ellen, huh, Bernard? What a story, huh?"

Rachel Kellerman intervened sharply. "Are we finished, Saul?" she asked. "Truly, are we finished? Or are we going to do a tour of the history of radicalism and its failure in every fucking state of the Union?"

Saul Kellerman grinned and opened up his hands, palms out, like a supplicant for mercy. Bernard squirmed in the silence that had fallen. He looked at Mary Ellen, who looked away from all of them.

"No, really" said Bernard, "I didn't know any of that. Really. That's interesting. For me. Really, uh, interesting Mr Kellerman."

"Saul, Bernard. Call me Saul, Bernard," said Saul Kellerman, avuncular and warm.

"Yeah, call him Saul, Burrn-aard," said Rachel Kellerman, cold and disdainful.

"Call him Saul, like he says. Maybe you'll get him further along the road to Damascus. He's already started out, haven't you, sweetie?"

The silence that fell over them reproached any well-meant attempt at conciliatory small talk. That would have only sunk them deeper into a disarray no conventional conversation could make cohere. Bernard looked, in a glance, at Mary Ellen who was stareing resolutely at a far wall splattered with unframed canvasses, four large Abstract works in oil, their glaring primary colours warding each other off in a pattern of triangles, squares and circles. Rachel Kellerman sat stock still except for a finger which wiggled around inside her empty glass where the ice cubes had dwindled to melt-water. Saul Kellerman had groaned out loud the moment she had stopped speaking. He stretched to his full, domineering height. Silently, sulkily, he began to stride across the room to the drinks cabinet. The unexpected silence was so strained it was almost unbearable. At least, it was so far as Bernard was concerned. He heard himself say:

"I think I know what you mean, though, Mr Kellerman. Saul, I mean. From where I come from, it's, in some ways anyway, not dissimilar. I mean, you see, I'm not from England. I'm not English. I'm from Wales. Welsh. From the valleys. South Wales. My father used to say that Aneurin Bevan, Nye, a socialist politician, from our South was attacked like that. Viciously. Called names. Like the Kingfish, perhaps."

The silence shifted a gear. It settled into a space open for negotiation. Kellerman stopped in full flight. He turned.

"Bev-anne," he said. "I know about him, for sure —National Health Service after the war. *Time* magazine put a likeness of him on its front cover at the time, with a scalpel in his mouth. An enemy of the Luce Foundation, and all its nefarious works, so one of the good guys. So, Bernard, you're from Wales. Why didn't you say?"

There came via Rachel Kellerman, the relief of laughter, inexplicable in origin except for its need, and it was gratefully taken up by a smiling Mary Ellen and a nodding Bernard who just repeated that indeed he was. Saul Kellerman cocked his head to his left and surveyed Bernard Jenkins anew.

"The South. That, then, Bernard, would be coal-mining country, wouldn't it? When I was in England in '44, waiting to ship out, we didn't get to see the sights, visit the country I mean, outside of London and, for me, Oxford once, but we knew, I knew, and some of my buddies, where you guys were. In Wales. Shit you guys even went on strike in the mines, didn't you, just before D-day. I remember that. You knew your rights, huh? Christ! I remember hoping they'd call the whole fuckin' thing off because of you guys. You Reds! You Commies!"

Saul Kellerman was delighted the way the talking between them was now going. Bonding. Communicating. Solidarity. His eyes urged Bernard on, so the Welshman said, "Saul, my own father was a coal miner actually. He was, uh, a striker, a communist, uh sympathiser."

"Fuckin' ace," said Kellerman. "This calls for a drink".

"Whooppee-do," said his wife and waggled her empty glass at him. Mary Ellen stirred, wanting to be part of the good news.

"You never told me that, Burr-naard," she said. "That you were from Way-uhls, yes. But not about the communism, no. Really?"

Bernard had become, in this company, suddenly of interest. He felt it. He liked it. He was, here and now, an exotic. He was the catalyst able to effect change. In mood. In understanding. In relationships. His backstory was extracted from him piece by previous piece, gently in case the thread would snap and their fascinated interest would not be able to spool on into sympathy, assurance, support. Mary Ellen decided she was supporter-in-chief by original claim to the territory marked Bernard Jenkins so that, by proxy, she could be an ersatz adjunct, a satellite to the dangerous cosmos of Kellerman ,with the suffocation of her genteel and purblind ancestry left in the wake of her daring. Daring to be there. With Jewish radicals. Daring to think for herself. Wrongs to be righted. Omigod, a Commie, too. Well sort of. Mary Ellen tried to look serious and to glow with an unknowing pridefulness, all at the same time. If she was with Bernard Jenkins she was, she must be, of interest to Saul Kellerman.

The great lawyer was feeding his witness the lines, the questions required to be put if the respondent was to come clean. Bernard was dredging his mind to find the precise answers the inquisitor really wanted to hear. He decided to keep it simple. Vague, but inspirational in general and with colour in the detail. So, generations before him, his great-great-grandfather, from west Wales originally, left the land

and back-breaking poverty to do back-breaking work, to the east, in the coal pits of the industrialised valleys, for wages. Marriage and family and a cohort of mining sons and coalminers' daughters followed on in a chronological wake. Rachel Kellerman said he described it so vividly, that she could see it. Could see it how it was, how she remembered seeing it, when she was sixteen, in the movies, crying when she saw John Ford's picture *How Green Was My Valley*. She said it had made her want to read the book. Maybe she would now finally get around to it. Now that she'd met Burr-naard, and touched the real thing. Bernard shuffled on his seat with the pleasure he was giving. Mary Ellen confessed she'd never seen the movie, never read the book. Saul Kellerman snorted and said Hollywood hocus-pocus. Bernard ploughed on.

Until him, he said, all the men in his family, his forbears, had worked underground. In the pits. Until him. He was the one who'd escaped. They'd wanted him to escape. Via grammar school and then to university. Or School, as you say he said, and smiled for them. His father had always been politically aware, he said, since the 1930s, like in Huey Long's day he added, and, well just naturally he guessed, supported the communists in the union. Not the Labor men? asked Saul. Bernard said, well yes that, too, broadly, but more than that, too, and nodded to himself. Saul helped with the detail. He mused about the Cold War, Suez, Hungary, CND, and so on. Bernard said that he was, of course, very young at the time and that his father had died, around four years ago, before he went off to School in England. That was tough, Rachel said, and her husband speculated under his breath – "Black lung, I bet" – but with such supressed vehemence that Bernard found the immanent sympathy of the three of them verging on a physical bond. He dropped his head, and let the silence, a better one this time, take over again. It seemed that his father had in this company, paid his dues for him.

* * * * *

At the dinner table a mood of self-reflected, communal glory settled over the entire party. Glory by the will-power of self-association. Saul Kellerman began to tell stories. Celebrity tales. Badmouth yarns. Loaded anecdotes. Mary Ellen had relaxed into laughter. Like Saul Kellerman she drank Chablis with her food, and unlike her host, found laughing, eating and drinking more and more demanding. Rachel drank only red wine, Gevrey Chambertin was what the label on the bottle told Bernard, and she ate silently and sparingly. Bernard had his crystal goblet filled to the brim with the garnet coloured wine , and he, in turns, admired and ate the thickly sliced turkey, the creamy coleslaw, the tangy cranberry sauce, the unusual (for him, he said) butternut squash and the sautéed rosemary-and-garlic potatoes. His blue-and-white china plate was piled high by Saul Kellerman, twice over, and he was sated both by the food before him and the admiring company with whom he sat. Dessert was to be apple-cobbler but the decision was to wait awhile, to rest, though not from drinking. That continued from the bottles Saul Kellerman had opened and placed around the table which he left in order to fetch, for him and Bernard, two cigars whose closed ends he snipped off from their plump tubes of fragrant leaf.

He rolled the cigars, one at a time, between his fingers and let them whisper in his ear. He sniffed the aroma of rot and decay. He gave one to Bernard. "Havana," he said. "A gift from Cuba." Then he said, "That bastard Kennedy." He lit the end of his cigar with the flame from a battered Zippo lighter and leaned across to light Bernard's cigar. He drew gently on his smouldering Havana and his guest watched and did the same. Puffs of smoke rose in blue whorls above their heads and flattened out into low clouds, pungent with ordure and the heady sweetness of black soil. Kellerman held his cigar in front of him. He contemplated its slow burn. It glowed with little, winking sparks of fire. It pulsated in his sturdy hand. Mary Ellen began to feel queasy.

Bernard puffed and sucked, and floated into an out-of-body giddiness. Saul Kellerman grew solemn.

"The thing is", he said, "that cunt, LBJ, for all his Texan chicanery, had more spunk than all of the Kennedys, a bunch of rich kids playing god, ever had. Civil rights? Johnson. Labour rights? Johnson. Poverty programmes? Johnson. Square deal, New Deal, Fair Deal? Johnson's in that line, not JFK. Take Vietnam away, Kennedy's poisonous legacy to him, and he knocks fuckin' Camelot into Kingdom Come. Yeah, something of ole' Huey Long about Lyndon, I think. We'll have to see. 1968 isn't too far away for him now. He'd better do his thing."

Kellerman put his cigar into the onyx ashtray his wife had brought to the table. Its smoke drifted upwards, a writhing column of waste.

Saul Kellerman had moved on to the pontificating state which was the counterpoint to his judgmental mode.

"Except. Except, of course. What of the common man? Black and white. What will they do for the common man, these bastards, eh Bernard? Nothing. Nothing. They'll have to do it for themselves. In your country, Bernard, in Wales maybe they got that. Maybe that's why your old man was a communist. People gotta do it for themselves, but it won't just happen. You know, if they can't, can't see it straight for now, they need a light to guide them, to help them, to stop them being such dumb, helpless bastards."

It was warm in the room in the open-plan house where the Kellermans lived. The sun was still beating its rays against the house's wrap-around windows. A central heating boiler in the basement had kicked in on its late November timer to increase the heat coming from the discreetly boxed-in wall radiators. Saul Kellerman and Bernard Jenkins had taken off their jackets and sat at the table with their shirt-sleeves rolled up above the wrist. Rachel Kellerman, alone, was untroubled by the warmth. Mary Ellen asked, her voice noticeably slurred, if she could have a glass of iced water. Bernard wanted the talk to be distributed amongst them, again, for it to return to the bonhomie, the conversational ease enjoyed earlier, when he, Bernard, had been centre stage in the Kellerman's open-plan house.

"I think, uh, Saul," he said "that we all have to, uh, find our own way."

The moment it was said, he knew that he meant it but that its meaning was not clear to him. Not yet.

"That's horse-shit, Burrn-aard" said Saul Kellerman, and he picked up his cigar and waggled it in front of his own red and looming face. He growled at Bernard. "Not everyone can be in a position to do that, or even to feel capable of it. That's the lie of the American fuckin' Dream. That they can. Truth is people get beaten down. People get fooled. People get fuckin' socially lobotomised. It's how the System works. Jesus, your old man knew that, kid."

Bernard looked at Mary Ellen whose face appeared translucently pale in the light. Rachel Kellerman took out another un-tipped cigarette and reached over the table for her husband's lighter. She looked quizzically at Bernard as if to elicit a response from him, or else see him be run over, be bulldozed by Saul Kellerman, like everyone he'd ever met. Bernard's response was a question.

"Perhaps not everyone is crushed?" he wondered. "Perhaps we all have, uh, an inner strength, one that only we know…" was as far as he got before Saul Kellerman began thumping the table.

"What is this? You been reading Reader's Digest, or the mottoes in Fortune Cookies, or something? Let me spell this out again for you Burrn-aard. People just get the juice sucked out of them."

Kellerman wet his lower lip with the tip of his tongue, a gesture of innocence and good faith, a sign of a yearning to have his point understood. He started again but more quietly, in a concerned, fraternal tone.

"Look, kid. Let's put it this way. Let me give you a-for-instance, Bernard. Two days ago, just before this Thanksgiving, I was in Manhattan for a conference-call with some slick, high-rolling

Attorneys, with whom I have, God-forgive me, sometimes have to associate. Doesn't matter what about, just to say I'd been in offices like theirs too many times for the good of my soul. Worked in them. Made filthy moolah in them. Mid-town, pre-war offices. Architecturally stunning inside and out. Get the picture, huh?

So, the meeting ends. It's on the sixteenth floor. I say less-than-happy goodbyes. Have a great Thanksgiving, and all that. I leave. I walk to the elevator. There is, of course, in buildings like this one, an elevator boy. Or, in this case, an elevator man. I press the button. The elevator arrives. The door opens. There's a gilded cage. It rolls back. I step in. I say 'Ground floor' before he can say anything. I don't look at him. I don't register whether he's a Negro, a Puerto Rican, young, old, white, yellow. He's a blank to me. All I'm doing is thinking of the sour end of the business I've been discussing for hours. He's operating the elevator. I'm riding in the elevator. We go down. I get out. I don't look at him. I don't thank him. Only, as I'm walking away, do I hear him thanking me and hoping I'll have a Nice Day. And, presumably, he goes back up. And down. And up. All and every Nice Day. Serving guys like me in our button-down Brooks Brothers shirts and Oxford brogues, and three fuckin' piece suits. And its only when I'm back on the train to Westchester, sitting at the bar with a large dry martini in front of me, only then Bernard, do I think of him. Don't ask me why. I dunno. But I did. And I feel ashamed. Ashamed of myself, of course, Bernard. But also, and here's the crunch, of him. What, in life, has led him to be this up-and-down, down-and-up, thank-you-so-much, servile clown?

He needs a wage? Ok, I can grant that. But, tell me, of this wage slave, where's a remnant of human dignity in what he does? In what he's forced by the System to do! Alone, for chrissake, alone in his cage. In his prison. For what? Eight hours at a time? It's soul-destroying. It's mindless. It's anonymous. It's without human worth. No end-in-sight. Just pressing buttons for people who could press them for themselves. And smiling, and thanking people like me. Just like a Step 'n Fetchit out of a Jim Crow South or off a Plantation like Mary Ellen's family probably once had, eh honey? And, oh sure, I coulda looked at him, smiled back, even thanked him. Maybe given him the tip he no doubt expected. And if I had, and this is my point, Bernard, and I'm sure it would've been your old man's, too, my point is that I'd have been colluding in his self-imprisonment, in his self-denial, in his self-sacrifice, in his own acceptance of his own-fate. People like the elevator man are vessels that need to be emptied of the shit that is drowning them from within. They have to be emptied before they can be filled up with new hopes, with the guts to help turn this awful American world upside-down. You do see, don't you?"

Saul Kellerman halted abruptly. His hands had not moved, but now he pulled them together and clasped them. His eyes were shining. He might have been tearful. Mary Ellen shuddered upright, her pallor now a mottled green. She staggered from the table. Her chair fell over. Rachel Kellerman said that it was back in the hallway, on the right, honey. Mary Ellen half-fell from the table, half-stumbled across the room. A door slammed. The indiscreet sound of gulping and vomiting came from the bathroom. A faucet was run as cover for the noise of Mary Ellen's condition. Drunk, and now sick with it. Bernard had kept his eyes on Saul Kellerman's unwontedly motionless hands all during the lawyer's closing statement. The noises-off, of choking and retching and gurgling, jolted him back to himself. Saul Kellerman was not expecting a reply to his rhetoric. What he was given was a riposte which made Rachel Kellerman sit up, and listen.

"What do you know what that guy feels? Or what he thinks? Or what he does outside that cage you put him in? You don't know. You said it yourself, you didn't even bother to talk to him. For you he's just an object, isn't he? But he's a subject, too, Mr Kellerman. An individual subject who thinks. Who feels. Who acts. He may not feel what you want him to feel. He may not think what you expect, you know. And he acts, perhaps, in the only way he can. He might even have been being ironic, have you thought of that?"

Bernard smeared a sticky hand across his mouth. Saul Kellerman decided to pity him.

"You're fuckin' romanticising the brain-dead, Burr-naard. Ok, he may not be able to entirely help that his cerebellum has become desiccated through society's abuse, but, there we are, as I said, it is."

"No. No", Bernard groaned. "That's where you are, Saul. Do you know if he goes home and listens to Beethoven? You do not. Or that he reads Dickens or poetry? You do not. You just judge. You don't look and you don't listen. And you don't really see. Other people are other, that's what you don't like"

"You can't really believe in any of that, can you? Of a guy like that? Up and down. Down and up. Well, do you Burrn-aard?"

"It's not important whether I do or not," Bernard told him. "Or whether it's true or not."

"Then it's even more horse-shit, my friend," Kellerman spat out at him.

"No. It's being human," said Bernard. "The human bit, Saul, and by the way you used to be right about my name. It is Bernard. The human part means that if the lift attendant was stupid, if he was illiterate, a philistine, a political know-nothing, whatever, he's still somebody, and that makes him something. That entitles him to your attention. Your respect even. Maybe for just not being you. For being himself. For being other. But you, at best, you turn him into an object of pity, a vessel to be filled with your good works, a project to be turned around. You care, Mr Kellerman, I acknowledge that. But you don't love, do you?"

"My, my, my," said Rachel Kellerman. Saul Kellerman glared at his wife. He said that this was a waste of his time. That he'd warned her they didn't know who these people were. The invitation was all her soft-hearted, do-gooding, liberal-thinking fault. Serve her right. And this Burrn-aard, or whatever his real name was, was a moralising rat-fink whose own father, if he could hear him, would be embarrassed at the way the religiose creep had turned out. Mention of his father gave Bernard a jolt, an instant's reflection on what his old man would really feel about what had been said and done that afternoon. He decided, and instantly too, that he knew what his father would have felt, and that he would never ask him. Bernard lowered his head. He bunched his fists.

Saul Kellerman grunted, out loud, that, Jesus H Christ, this was a sorry excuse for the son of a Welsh coalminer. He pushed his chair away from the table. He walked to the glass wall that led to the garden and slid open a partition door. He stumbled through it and onto the lawn which sloped imperceptibly towards the unseen ocean. He did not close the door. Rachel Kellerman opened her mouth to speak. She stopped when Mary Ellen re-appeared and lurched towards the open door, whispering something about needing some fresh air and being back soon. She walked hesitatingly, vaguely, towards Saul Kellerman who turned at her approach, and her saying his name. He said something back to her, and she leaned into him. He seemed to Rachel Kellerman and Bernard Jenkins to be holding her up. He had his long arms across her sunken shoulders. He eased her slowly down the path to the copse at the garden's end, the dark wood beyond which the ocean lapped the shore. Bernard squinted into the distance as the two figures became lost to sight. He half-rose from his chair. Rachel Kellerman placed tapered fingers on his hand and stroked it. She said, "Hey, don't worry. Whatever else, Saul is not like that. Trust me on this. He'll just be talking," and she poured them both another glass of Gevrey Chambertin. She clinked her glass against his. She said to Bernard Jenkins, "Come on, Burrn-aard, I'll show you something."

In a far recess on the left-hand side of the room in Rachel Kellerman's open plan home was a wooden railed-off section near the book-cased wall. Within that smaller space was a cast-iron spiral stair, a dozen or so steps, which went down into a den. Saul Kellerman's private space. His wife went down the stairs first, beckoning Bernard on and down into a square cement-walled study with no windows. Books lined three walls from floor to ceiling. On the fourth wall were framed photographs of Saul Kellerman. Kellerman shaking hands with released and relieved clients. Kellerman with famous faces in restaurants, in bars, on public platforms. There were framed newspaper reports of trials, and mis-trials. There were signed letters of thanks and of commendation. There were framed Degree diplomas, from City University of New York and from Harvard Law School. There were no photographs of Rachel Kellerman on the wall, or on the old-fashioned knee-hole desk that squatted, with its wooden Captain's chair, in the centre of the room underneath its one, hanging light. Rachel Kellerman made a half-circle with her arms and pirouetted around the desk. She said, "This is Saul. This, Burrn-aard, is what you need to understand. A kid from the Bronx. From a poor neighbourhood even for the Bronx. A tough neighbourhood. His father was first-generation American. From Lithuania. His mother the same, just a boat or so before him. A living from peddling, from push-carts, around the streets. Then as a tailor. Saul, a stand-out 'A' student in High School. Scholarships to City University in New York, then, wow! to Harvard. See what I mean. He's a decorated war hero. A stellar career at the Bar. Me, I guess. What's not to like, huh, Burrn-aard? What's not to like, you tell me."

She had been carrying her wine glass with her. She put it down on her husband's desk. She leaned back against it, and looked wistful, and, Bernard Jenkins thought, quite lovely. He swayed, a little drunkenly, nearer to her. Rachel Kellerman looked at him. She pointed an index finger at him.

"So here's the grift , Bernie boy. He wants to go back to it all. To leave Mamaroneck in Westchester County. To leave all this. To live in the Bronx. Again. To work pro bono. To take the cases no-one else dares to take on. For why? Because he's one of the good guys and some days a fuckin' saint? Well, yeah. Yes. He actually is. I guess. But also because he's decided that the whole wide American world, and its fouled up Dream, the one his parents thought he'd made his own, makes him, in fact, sick with its lies, its corruption, its wickedness, its greed. Sick to death maybe. Certainly sick to the point of madness. He thinks the apocalypse is coming. The revolution alone can stop it. Maybe before this decade is done. So, no time for sympathy, Burrn-aard. No time for fellow-feeling. No time for love. No time for me. Or anyone else."

Bernard Jenkins sensed a button was being pushed. No, he knew it, positively. It was his button. He felt sure of it. He took another step towards Rachel Kellerman. He reached out for her. But he was wrong, about her push if not about his button. Not unkindly, she laughed softly and pushed his hands away. It was a halt in proceedings.

"Hey, Burrn-aard, sweetheart," she said. "I'm sorry. I didn't mean… you know. We're not in the movies here, Ok? I only thought you needed to see for yourself what's going on, in him, from down here to up there, in his head. What's happening with Saul is big. Bigger than you, or Mary Ellen, or, from these days on, even me. See, I'm not going back with him. I haven't said it yet, but he knows. This is what it's all about today. And tomorrow he'll know, again, in his heart that he's right, that the rest of us, me included, are in the wrong. You disappointed him, is all. He'll be being nice old Saul to your girl right now, and when he comes back in, he'll be fine with you. You're right, he does care."

"She's not my girl," said Bernard Jenkins. Rachel Kellerman sighed. She picked up her glass, and drained it. She walked back up the stairs to the living room of their open plan house. Saul Kellerman and Mary Ellen were sat on the buttercup-yellow sofa. He said that Mary Ellen would like to go home, and he said sorry to Bernard if he'd been a bit rough on him. He assured his wife that he was okay to drive. It wasn't far. Light traffic on the road at this time. If they hurried they could catch the 5.55 train to the city.

* * * * *

Dr Bernard Jenkins, sixty year old CEO Europe of Tunnel Fabrication Worldwide, sat reading his up-market tabloid newspaper on his daily train commute. He chose the tabloid format so he could turn the pages even when hemmed in on all sides by sitting and standing rail passengers. He had done the journey for the last ten years, after his transfer from Geneva and promotion to CEO Europe. Fifteen minutes by car, from his detached, sprawling Tudor farmhouse conversion, to park at the station and catch the train. Forty minutes on the train to London. Then twenty minutes, max, if the traffic was light, by black cab to his office. Clockwork if everything was on time, and with a seat at the train window time, too, to read the Monday paper.

He read it methodically, from front to back. Endless speculation about the feud between Blair and Brown in the dying days of New Labour. Leaks and counter-claims. Too many Christians in that cabinet, Bernard had said often enough to his wife. You watch, he'd said, self-righteous pomposity and self-justifying belief in being infallible will follow on. He took no satisfaction when it did. After over three decades dealing with governments and their officials across the globe, Bernard Jenkins, CEO, distrusted all moralising and hand-wringing from whichever political quarter it came. The central section of the paper was the sad narrative of military intervention without a social strategy, and then acting without any historical or cultural grasp. Bloody lawyers, Bernard thought. No business would act like that. Certainly not the ones he'd worked successfully for, often in fraught and delicate circumstances.

He reached the Sports pages, skipping the Register and Obit columns, with relief. He checked for the lower division Welsh club rugby results, followed at a distance but still more meaningful to him than the artificially constructed so-called "Regions" back home. More bone-headed lack of understanding, he'd informed his Surrey drinking cronies in the golf club he attended for the company, in both senses, not for the playing on the greens. He read the soccer match reports and the tedious player-profiles. He'd exhausted the paper after less than twenty minutes. He looked out of the window. He glanced at his fellow passengers and looked away in the same manner they did if eyes should meet. The English, he thought. What decent people. By and large. The English. What a furtive bunch. This lot anyway. Different elsewhere. He fiddled with the paper in his hands. He opened it again, to the obituary pages. Last thing left to read. Appropriately enough, he thought.

There was a full page obituary notice for some distinguished Second World War soldier who had later retired as a Brigadier General to farm in Rhodesia, and then home to Scotland to hold non-executive posts in public utilities, and stand, without success, for Parliament. He read every word and looked at the full-length oil portrait which had been used of a young man in tartan-trousered uniform instead of any later photograph. Typical spin, Bernard thought as he turned the page. The second obituary had a photograph but only half a page's summation of the life. The photograph was also not particularly recent. It was of the upper body, head and shoulders, of someone walking away, fast down the street, but turning back to shout something at the newspaper cameraman. It was, for Bernard, recognisably an older Saul Kellerman, and the headline merely confirmed it:

Saul Kellerman. American radical lawyer and Civil Rights Activist.

The piece was more factual than considered. The facts and nothing but the facts. As if, thought Bernard Jenkins.

Saul Kellerman had been found dead by a neighbour in his walk-up, cold water apartment in the Bronx, New York City. A suspected heart attack. He was in his seventy ninth year. He lived alone. Divorced from his only wife, Rachel, nee Weiss, Kellerman in 1972. She survived him. There had been no children. Rachel Kellerman, contacted in a retirement home in Florida, said, "Saul had always had a big, big heart. It was never broken by anything, or anybody. It just stopped, I guess."

The rest of the mini-essay was a bare bones account of his career. How a well-respected and well-heeled attorney had left his practice to plead the cases of Freedom Riders in the racially segregated Deep South in the early 1960s. How he'd rapidly became the lawyer of, the advocate for, any and every dissident voice which was raised against established forces in that riven America of the 1960s. He defended those others, even those perceived to be terrorists and traitors. He sided with the disaffected and the dangerous, from the Black Panthers to the Weathermen, and in 1968 he was in Chicago with the anti-war protesters and in jail with Mailer. In the law courts of the land he was as forensic as he was fearless, more and more challenging of the legal right to try his clients, for their alleged crimes, at all. For some he had morphed into an egotistical, publicity seeking monster. The obituary notice quoted one academic jurist, by no means the most unkind of his critics, as labelling Kellerman, 'The man who forsook American Altruism for Un-American Ultraism'.

Saul Kellerman had never retreated from his self-declared war on American power. If the state accused, Kellerman defended. Anti-war rioters. Bomb-makers. Mobsters. Confessed killers. Saul Kellerman had proclaimed that in the spider-webbery of corporate greed and imperial dominion there was no justifiably assignable guilt for those who had, necessarily, to stand up or be crushed, to devour or be devoured. The obituary said that, even after some years of relative quiescence in his old age, Kellerman had remained a lightning rod for divisive opinion in America. To his admirers he was a Patriot. In the eyes of his enemies he was a Demagogue-run-amok.

Bernard Jenkins closed his newspaper. In his memory, from what he knew, Saul Kellerman was neither of those things. Or not completely so. Or, if both, then, he thought, like Saul's admired Huey Long, the one thing as necessary to be the desired other. The train entered a tunnel. He looked at his reflection, suddenly there before him within the darkened window pane of the train. He grimaced at his rounded-out face. At his wispy hair. Grey and white, he knew, and thinning on top. He thought now, of course, of Mary Ellen Robinson who had written to him for a while after she'd gone back to Baton Rouge, Louisiana, to work in a pro-bono law firm as a junior partner. She'd married another law partner, older than her, from within the firm. He'd written to Bernard, five years into their marriage and after she'd died in a car crash on her way to plead a case in New Orleans against the arraignment of a black teenager for robbery. He thought of Rachel Kellerman, who'd never been in the movies. And he thought, as he had many times over the years that had since passed, of Saul Kellerman who had remained the most disturbing, the largest man, in every sense, he had ever met. He re-played in his mind the dispute they had had at Thanksgiving in 1966, and he wondered if Saul Kellerman had ever puzzled over the nub of it, had ever considered the real cause of it, of Bernard's outburst. His dissent. His shame. He stared at himself in the blackened window until the train came out of the tunnel, and the reflection abruptly vanished though his self-reflexive mood remained.

It had been a long time since he had thought, as he now did, of his father. A quiet, resolute man who had worked from the age of fourteen, throughout the Depression years in the coalfield, in the village's co-operative wholesale store. He worked there until his death, at sixty-five, soon after his retirement, and only five years after Bernard had returned from America. He had risen in the co-op from floor-sweeper and grocery-boy to run the Gents' haberdashery floor where he measured the inside-legs of colliers and tugged the Sunday-best suit jackets of miners tight at their muscled backs. He had married late so he was in his forties and his wife, a spinster until then, in her mid-thirties when Bernard was born. They had met in and were married from Moriah Baptist Chapel. He had saved his wages to buy, freehold, a small terraced house where the couple went to live. Life for them was patterned by the security of routine. The same meals, rotated around the same weekdays and with the ritual of cooked dinners on Sundays, marked out all their lives as regularly as the tick of their kitchen clock. His father potched about in his garden shed. His father worked an allotment in a waistcoat with his shirt-sleeves rolled up. His father was moderate and friendly on Saturday nights in the British Legion club. His father kept his opinions, on politics and on religion, discreetly to himself. Where he could not be honest and open, he chose to be silent. Bernard knew that his father loved both him, and his mother Crid, more deeply than he could ever express, beyond a hug. He knew that they literally adored him, and that his father's pride in his son's accomplished success in the world was boundless. He knew that his father would have forgiven him his lapse, and he also knew that he, Bernard Jenkins, was right to feel ashamed throughout his life.

With his train slowing down to pull into Waterloo, Bernard was silently repeating to himself the last words which Saul Kellerman had shouted out to him as that other commuter train, of almost forty years before, had departed Mamaroneck, Westchester County for Manhattan and his future life.

"Take a chance, kid" he had yelled, so loudly that others on the platform had turned around to look at him, their surprised attention pulled towards him by his urgency, his fervour, his being, in every way larger-than-themselves.

"Take that chance, Bernard," he'd shouted. "It only comes the once. Don't ever forget. Here and now is always forever. Take that chance."

He hadn't though, he thought. Taken the chance. Whatever it might have been. Bernard knew he had settled for something else. He was still not sure, in the here and now, if it was the lesser thing for which he had plumped. Only that it was different, and certainly not what Saul Kellerman had envisioned. For himself. For Bernard. For everyone. But there again Bernard reflected, as he walked swiftly through the station's Terminus, when that other commuter train had pulled away, leaving Saul Kellerman in its wake, it had not yet been 1968. It was certainly not 1968 now, he acknowledged to himself, as he hailed a taxi at the one right spot on the road outside where he knew to go to avoid queuing in the station with all the other commuters. Perhaps it had never been 1968. Not for Bernard Jenkins anyway.

Inter Nationals

Inside the painted lines. Red and white lines. Marking the boundaries of touch. Out of touch. In touch. In play. Trainers squeaking on the scuffed gymnasium floor of the university sports centre. Not leisure. Pain more like. For Gavin anyway. The youngest and the softest. Out of school and unchained from the desk of a scholarship boy. Liberated by pain. By exercise. "Mens sana in corpore sano", the Latin scholar intoned to himself as he was urged to run and run. "Come on you fat bastard. Run. Come on!" Just to get into position. Just to touch the ball. Momentarily. To lose the ball. "Oh, for fuck's sake, Gav!" To stop. Panting. As the ball is thumped past him. Again. Into the centre circle. To their player. Big bloke, hefty, making to control the bounce. Too late. Jimmy takes the ball off the big bloke's toe. His body swerves away from an incoming tackle. He spurts down the centre. Towards the goal. He shimmies to the left. He shifts his balance to the right. He shoots. Hard and scuddingly low. And, goal! Gavin hadn't moved. The other three clap Jimmy on the back. Their star player. He grins at Gavin who grins back, still panting. Elated. Friday night. With lager and curry to come. Five-a-side football.

And, shit, they were off again. Gavin once more by-passed by pace and skill. But still running. Content to be with them. Happy, in fact, to be one of them. Tolerated. No, accepted. Encouraged. Clumsiness irrelevant here. Only five-a-side after all. Bit of a kick-about. Students. Gavin, just up from home, at eighteen, to read Classics to his parents' uncomprehending consternation. Big Mac from Belfast, graduating in Civil Engineering at the end of the year. Ed, the Yank, a PhD in Tudor Parliamentary History, on the wing. Selçuk, from Ankara, a second degree in Management and Business, buzzing around in mid-field.

And Jimmy of course. Jimmy, the mature age student, at thirty-six too old for the full game but made for five-a-side. Jimmy, redundant steel worker, from the blast furnaces. A nugget of a man. Gavin's idol. Gavin's friend. The one who'd brought him in – "Us Taffs got to stick together up 'ere, butt!" – just to make up the numbers. He'd hesitated. He'd never played. All that heads-down, exam upon exam, "O" to "A", and his pudgy fingers dented by holding a pen for scribbling hours on end, and his body, soft and cosseted, just an appendage of his force-fed mind. "Mens" stretched and exercised to a fierce sharpness. "Corpus" left behind as a mere foil to that edged weapon. Still, only five-a-side, and companionship – so, Gavin had said he'd "give it a go".

To buy: black football shorts, white T-shirts, red-and-green striped trainers. Under Jimmy's cajoling the drench of sweat – the ache of calf muscles for the first time – tensing, strengthening – more pliable – feeling his body – able to run, if not to play. Pleased for any praise – especially from Jimmy. Simplicity. Support. Words to take to sleep – "Eh, well played, butt" – to dream of the game. The one which had gone. The one yet to come. Waiting through the week for Friday. And the Friday after that – through the autumn – into the winter. The easiness, for him, of lectures and essays now counterpointed, for him, by the challenge of the university sports centre on Friday nights. His unspoken objective to be played out between two white goalposted nets, sawn off and yellow meshed, at either end of the gym – frantic – exhausting – demanding. His objective, unspoken, was to score – one day. A goal. To score. For himself. For the team. For Jimmy.

There was a rhythm to it. He had begun to feel it. It was not intuitive with him. More a work of detection. Not his to share, but his now to appreciate, to sense as a possibility. It unfolded. Each time, a repetition. Each time, a different emphasis. The ball rolled out along the floor from the back. Mac to Ed's left foot on the right wing. Ed taps it sideways to Selçuk, and moves on, past half way. Selçuk looks up, doesn't risk a one-two with Gav on his left. Instead, he twists out of a tackle. Squares the ball, but jerkily, to Jimmy. And then, Gavin could see, everything stops, and somehow everything starts up again – in an instant. The stuttering syncopation of pass-and-go is halted by Jimmy's pause. It is an actual stop, a stand still, foot-on-the-ball moment. All the players seem transfixed, frozen. Jimmy walks the ball, just a pace or two, in front of him. Then the mood he employs is, without warning, percussive. He seems attached to the ball, and man and object accelerate as one. Jimmy is stocky, low slung and crouching, his speed and his body mass combine to shield the ball, to whip it away by inches from desperate tackles. Despairing lunges. On the edge of the penalty area. Makes to shoot. Only the goalie to beat. And Jimmy shouts, "Eh, Gav, d'you want this one? Wanna score it?", and stops to glance to the left of the area where Gavin has run, and waits. For the pass. For the goal. To score. Against the goalie who has shuttled his feet to the right, in anticipation, mistaken anticipation, as Jimmy sidefoots the ball into the net. Laughing. The goalie splay-footed, beaten by the ruse. Gav looks shamefaced. Gav looks delighted. Jimmy had said, "Well done, Gav. You made that goal, butt, you made it."

Afterwards. Over the pints. That was the theme tune. They played it over and over. Gav the Dummy Runner. Gav the Decoy. Gav the Blindside. Gav and the Game Plan. Gav the False No. 9. Jimmy had to explain that one to Ed. Gav thought he was Gav the Lucky Bugger. All this from that chance meeting over coffee in the student refectory when Jimmy had heard his accent. Not Jimmy's Swansea scattergun of liquid vowels and slurred end-consonants, but linked enough despite Gavin's educated and parentally guided vocal removal from the sound of the streets all around. Gavin had never met anyone like Jimmy. The same city, but suburban semi-det to terraced three-up-three-down. Might as well have been closed off from each other by unbreakable, immoveable, partitions of plate glass. Jimmy, though, was complete. For Gavin this made him a source of freedom, something as yet over the horizon, beyond his experience and, until now, his aspiration.

Jimmy was senior. Jimmy was mentor. Jimmy was married. Jimmy was playing away. Jimmy was liberation-on-legs. Jimmy teased and tantalised. About girls. About drinking. About life. Gavin took it all in and vowed to play catch up, one day soon. It was enough that Jimmy knew how. "I'm old enough to be your father, butt", Jimmy told him; and "Tell me again, what's your mother's maiden name? … Never! Well, then I could be, after all, see Gav!" And, with the others listening, Gavin laughed, too, just at the thought of it.

Jimmy was "doing", as he put it, Politics. But there again, at least so far as practice and experience was concerned, he seemed to Gavin to be already complete. The stories Jimmy told were rifted with veins of indignant anger and passion. The customary rhetorical mode which might have been expected was undercut by anecdote, and the sly humour of which Jimmy was a master. From apprenticeship to section leader, from strikes to lay offs, from marches held in whichever cause was current to WEA classes held in worktime by union and management agreement, Jimmy placed himself at the centre of two decades of industrial strife. It was only actual political activity, conventional or maverick or both, which Jimmy had avoided. It was a "generational thing, butt", he'd shrugged. "Not for me, see", was his only explanation. It was as if the game of political activity and not the context was all that engaged him. Besides there was, he explained, "Only so much you can do with one body, know what I mean, butt, what with a few little dalliances and the soccer and all." Jimmy claimed that his wife had understood even if "OK, they'd separated a bit, for a bit. Took the two girls to her mother's, see butt, for a bit. While I do this course, see." He'd long fancied "using his brain-box properly" and the grants available for mature age students were too good to turn down, alongside the redundancy package he'd taken. "Fresh start, butt, and why not?"

In the months that followed the beginning of the autumn term in which they'd met, Gavin helped with the essay assignments at which, though he did do the reading, Jimmy baulked. "Can't seem to kick off, butt" he'd say, and Gavin worked on the structure, the sentence sense, the spelling, the general analytical focus from alpha to omega which Jimmy's raft of assembled ideas lacked if it was ever to float. Gavin felt privileged to help, and though neither man quite expressed it as such it was, between them, an inverse image of what happened every Friday night. The tyro footballer was the controller on the page, and the crack player struggled with the fluidity of ideas transposed into the formality of the written word. But together, Gavin thought, together, it's a team effort in the end. No difference.

The team which played together stayed together. That, Gavin could see, was the bargain to make and to keep. After the Christmas break they all came back together. Only Gavin had actually gone home for any length of time, and he decided, to parental surprise, to return early to the university. Needed to work at a few things, he'd told them. The team held practice sessions. They improved as a unit. When they started to play again they moved swiftly up the internal league of the scratch teams who met for friendly competition. Individual skills were sharpened. Gavin did one-to-ones with Jimmy on Tuesdays and Thursdays after essay-writing sessions. He learned how to cushion the ball. He learned how to trap and give the ball in one movement. He learned how to time a run to get into position. He learned how to wrap his foot around the ball to curl its intended path. He learned how to jump out of a tackle and still retain the ball. He learned how to shield the ball with his body. He learned how to bump an opponent to win the ball. He learned how to volley a ball on the rise. He learned how to shoot to keep the trajectory of the ball low. He learned how, in theory anyway, he might one day put the ball into the net to score. A goal.

In Jimmy's shadow, he felt his ability grow even if he would never blossom into something beyond the mechanics of the process. Through sheer effort he became, with his lurching runs and youthful energy, a part, a real if lesser part of the whole of the team. Not the liability to avoid, the passenger along for the ride provided by others, but a proper helper, a team player, able to contribute. Now, if he still never looked likely to score, yet he never lost the ball easily either, and would always tussle for it, run back to retrieve it, look to spoil the play of any opponent who, Jimmy would say, "Robbed you naked there, butt. Got to get it back, then." Gavin found his own voice, too. The tippy-tappy play-for-fun of most teams meant grunts and yells were rarely in order. Gavin discovered for himself the power of such intimidation, noise from nowhere, laced with the swearing and cursing Jimmy had taught him, even to the disruptive point of shoving and fouling. Not that Jimmy, elegant and powerful, ever resorted to that, but he vocally approved of his apprentice's newly tempered steel, and swiftly intervened to protect him from those who did not like the aggression of "Gavin the clogger", as Jimmy fondly christened him afterwards in the bar.

By the end of February the team were clear leaders. Top of their league's ladder board. Jimmy spent more and more time, often on his own, burnishing the skills he'd first displayed when younger on the muddy recreation grounds of rival work teams and village clubs, to deploy them again in what was, for him, the child-like dimensions of a five-a-side knock-about. When Jimmy turned it on, they all said with glee, he just "scores when he wants". And, as the university year passed, for his own satisfaction, he seemed to want to do that more and more.

It was in mid-March that Alfredo, an Argentinian medic, a trainee cardiologist in his early thirties, so just a few years younger than Jimmy, turned up. Ostensibly to watch. He had a studious air. He was bald. He wore round gold-rimmed glasses. He had on a pale blue and white striped Argentinian international shirt, buttoned to the neck, and black tracksuit bottoms above silver and blue training shoes. He was the first one ever who had come to watch them play. They could see him on the balcony above them where, as league leaders, they thrashed a rival, four nil, over two fifteen minute halves. Jimmy had scored all the goals.

At the end of the match, Alfredo came down to the hall and walked onto its sprung-floored pitch. He walked past Gavin who was still bent double, and gasping. He walked by Ed and Mac who were going off to shower. He walked over to the centre where Selçuk had draped an arm over Jimmy's shoulder to congratulate him. It was only to Jimmy that Alfredo wished to speak. He spoke softly, insistently, fluently, to tell Jimmy that he, Alfredo, was the captain of the university's five-a-side team, the best players from the various colleges, and that he had heard from others of Jimmy's prowess, and that also he could say now that he had seen it for himself. He said that he, Alfredo, had played, once or twice, for Boca Juniors in Buenos Aires, and often for their second team as his medical studies took him away from the professional game. He said that his team needed to recruit a reliable goal scorer to complement them, and in particular Alfredo's style of play, and that, from what he'd seen, he wanted Jimmy to play for the All Star university team, a team of true international quality. The All Stars had played other universities all across the country. All expenses were paid. They were about to enter the most important part of the season, a rolling series of play-offs to the domestic final, then a tournament in Paris, as a grand finale, and then possibly the European final itself. If he joined, Alfredo said, Jimmy would be playing with some players who were, like him, "Extra". Then he finished, and put his hands on his hips waiting for Jimmy's grateful acceptance. Instead, Jimmy told him, "Ta. But we're doing all right as it is, butt", that he was "enjoying himself, like", but didn't need "any extra aggro, what with essays and exams coming up, and stuff", so "thanks for asking, butt, but no thanks all the same." Alfredo said no more. He walked away. Gavin asked what he'd wanted. Jimmy ran his fingers through the plastered tangle of his greying hair and clapped Gavin around his shoulders to guide him to the changing room, and out of there. "Nothing much, butt", he said. "Latins, see. They all think they're toffee."

* * * * *

The following Friday when they trotted out of the changing room to play, it was Gavin who nudged Jimmy to look who was on the opposing team, one they'd beaten easily, but in a different guise, back in December. It was, dressed as before but without the gold-rimmed spectacles, the tall, willowy figure of Alfredo. Jimmy grinned widely. He went straight across to him and shook Alfredo's outstretched hand, and Jimmy said, "Well, okay then, butt, we'll see what you've got, eh?"

What followed was a masterclass. Whenever Alfredo had the ball – supported to his left and right by two other imports to his makeshift team – it would be as if the pattern of play, especially any rush and thrust, would be suspended whilst he decided on one of any several options he might choose. A mazy dribble. A splitting pass to take out two flatfooted and slower-witted opponents. Usually Gavin and Selçuk. An outrageous back-pass when on the run. A speculative shot from distance that stung Mac's hands. More often than not, a pivot from a central position to radiate the ball out and into the paths of his willing acolytes who Gavin, despairingly and futilely, chased and chased. Ed and Selçuk harried as best they could, the runners who were cued to bear down on Big Mac who saved and parried. Without any ball to use, Jimmy was the one to be by-passed, shut out of the game no matter how many times he snatched at the ball. But he never stopped grinning or talking. Mostly to Alfredo, who neither smiled nor replied back to him. The ball was sprayed imperiously from the feet of Alfredo, always playing with his head up to find that passage of play with which his control of the ball could do most harm. Before five minutes had gone Alfredo's team had scored twice.

From the re-start after the second goal, Jimmy took the ball on himself and, for once in the contest, his speed off the mark took him past the watchful guards stationed for defensive duty by the game's generalissimo, Alfredo. From the apex of his direct route to goal, Jimmy let fly. The ball arrowed into the top left hand corner of the net with such force that it ricocheted back out and into the goalscorer's path. Jimmy picked up the ball and handed it to the maestro who had come to show him how the game should be played. But it was Jimmy who now decided to deliver another lesson. He no longer stood off Alfredo, he buzzed around him, with or without the ball in the Argentinian's possession, and he cut off the avenues available for the passing game by jostling and darting at the pass-master. Alfredo tried to be even more commanding. Strategy against the merely tactical. He took up a deeper position, right in front of his goal, and instructed his runners to stand further away from him. This made it easier for Ed and Selçuk to stay back to man mark them. Gavin, in all this, scurried about, demented and irrelevant in this chess game of a football match. Whenever Jimmy managed to get on the ball after a move broke down, Alfredo's team retreated as one. Whenever Alfredo had any time to dictate play his drilled team moved up in close formation. As a team they were clearly superior. It was only a matter of time, and Gavin could see that that time was nearly there, that Jimmy could not do this, could not win it, by himself.

The team turned around, without a break, for the second half of fifteen minutes to come. It was still only 2-1 but the impetus was all one way. Gavin, for the first time in his life, felt physically overwrought with frustration at his own inadequacy. He had been made lesser again, only able to watch, yet not motionless, as the heavy rubberised football pinged and bounced and swerved, and was blocked and checked by bodies running on sheer willpower. Then, as if a string had snapped, the football went loose, unexpectedly slicing off Alfredo's silver and blue trainers and into the stride of an advancing Jimmy who swept past the tackle and shot on goal. It was almost too clean a hit. It went through the goalkeeper's open hands only to smash itself against the junction point of crossbar and post. It went back into play without touching the ground, right to the feet of Alfredo who was facing his own goal. He trapped it instantly and spun away with it, guiding the ball before him, at speed, downfield to the half-way line before a visceral scream of pain from behind caused him to hesitate. Another instant. It was Gavin who barrelled in on the playmaker and stuck out an ungainly heel which dislodged the ball. The ball spun on its axis, no longer controlled, anymore than was the bulky figure of Gavin who rotated with it through almost 360°, stretched for it with his right leg as it squirmed beyond him, and smacked it, first time, with the distended top of his foot, hard and scuddingly low from the half-way line. The ball skidded just in front of the stooping keeper, and went into the net on the unstoppable arc of its late rise. Goal. 2-2.

"Bloody hell, Gav. You've bloody well scored! Goal!" It was Jimmy. Gavin heard him from the ground where he lay. He had not seen the ball enter the net. He knew the moment he had connected, however, that he would score. He had felt, for the only time, an exquisite unity between his intent and the outcome of the action he had taken. He felt, instantaneously, complete in a manner he'd never experienced until the moment he had over-extended his right leg to follow through with the shot he had truly lined up on goal. Goal! He'd scored. He'd mastered the ball. And now he was flat out on the floor. His right leg, his short, pumped-up right leg, was stuck out in front of him. He was in gnawing pain. A toothache of epic, recurring pain in his leg, at the back of the knee. He tried to get up. He was hurting. He could not shift. Jimmy pulled him to a sitting position and Gavin cried out "No. No", in an agony he'd also never experienced, as if his body, not just his leg, had been torn apart. Someone tried to lift him by his armpits, but Alfredo said not to do so. He said, impassively and with the quiet accuracy of the certain, that it would be the hamstring. Stretched rather than snapped. Snapped would have been better, he said. Stretched would mean bed cure, rest with feet up, bouts of physio, for weeks and weeks. They picked him up as a foursome, holding his legs out and steady as Gavin gritted his teeth and moaned. They put him down, half sitting and half lolling on a bench at the side. Alfredo fetched some heavy duty painkillers and a glass of water. He patted Gavin solicitously on his arm. There would be need, shortly, to take him to A and E for examination but, first, to be calm. So to finish, why not, the game. He suggested that he and Jimmy play in a team of four against five. Jimmy asked Gavin if he could manage to hang on. Gavin nodded, and Gavin watched.

Alfredo and Jimmy played with brio, and in another spectrum of possibility. They did not so much find room to create, they created the room in which their talents could play. In that sense they were unplayable. They became not the expression of anything but the thing itself. This was physical literacy. It was graphic numeracy. It was instinctive. It was designed. It was a dance. It was telepathic in its movement and its dimensions. Jimmy would halt, stock still, then Jimmy would move like a fly eater's tongue to pick up the ball which Alfredo would release at the split second no-one else could touch its flight. Nor would Jimmy have been able to snap it up unless he had not anticipated, without being told or had signalled, the precise bi-section of time and space energised by Alfredo. Or else, Jimmy would taunt with sublime ball trickery, from instep to instep, until an opponent stepped into his trap and Jimmy walked out of it by laying-off the ball, almost as a caress, into the lengthening stride of Alfredo who drove on and shot to score, or, more often, devised an outrageous wall-to-wall piece of play with his partner, before one or other of them would score.

Partners were indeed what they were – short-term acquaintances with lifelong attraction. Gavin saw it immediately. He felt a leaden thud in his chest that was a duller and more prolonged pain than the nerve-twanging agony throbbing in his right leg. His leg remained doubled up at the knee. He could not uncoil it. He held the back of his knee with his right hand and the saliva dried up in his mouth. On the floor Ed and Selçuk and two A.N.Others were being run ragged. Yet, for them, there was no fear of such competition. To be so out-classed was almost a joy for such true amateurs. In goal Big Mac could applaud the regularity with which he was being beaten. It was an exhibition of supreme individuality which left the concept of a team in its wake. Except for Gavin, for whom something more than the team was unravelling along with the team and that was an ethos, a togetherness, the making of a whole from its parts, from its lesser parts. Meaning, he knew, himself.

He knew, too, that it was undeniable that Jimmy was revelling in this bestowed pomp. He was refreshed. He was truly fulfilled. His ability was on full display at last, and orchestrated by Alfredo it was irresistible. The goals they scored were almost an afterthought. They were only using the occasion and the presence of others as a backdrop to the footballing congress, the inter relationship between nationals, which they had found for themselves, and which was not available to others. When it was over, Alfredo finally smiled. Jimmy punched Alfredo on the upper arm. He was an All Star all right. It was clear that five-a-side on a Friday night was all over for Jimmy. And over, too, for Gavin who would not be able to play again anytime soon.

"It'll take time, butt", said Jimmy in the University Hospital's A and E department where they'd taken Gavin, carried between them, and in and out of Alfredo's car. A grumpy, elderly doctor had examined Gavin. Alfredo's instant diagnosis was confirmed. He was to rest in bed, with painkillers, and no exercise for a few weeks, then on crutches, with intense physio to take his elasticated parts back into their more flexible mode. It would take time. But, first, he would need, said the senior doctor, to have a Robert Jones. This turned out to be a bandaging technique named after the Welsh orthopaedic surgeon who had devised it. The leg was swathed, above and below the knee, in layer upon layer of tightly wrapped bandages which served to keep the leg rigid in its semi-bent position. Robert Jones was credited with saving many lives in the First World War with this ingenious splint of a field dressing to allow wounds and fractures to heal, as it would Gavin's lesser problem. It looked, he thought, propped up in bed, as ludicrous as that of any cartoon character he'd ever seen as a boy. He ate his grapes and read his books, and wondered about the efficacy of the Classics as a career in the late twentieth century world.

In May the All Stars, having conquered all before them at home, won in the European final in Paris. Jimmy scored the winning goal. 3-2. Alfredo hoisted the cup. The picture made the *Buenos Aires Herald*. Gavin had not travelled with Ed, Selçuk and Mac to see the game. He pleaded revision for his first year exams, which he passed with comfort. Jimmy came back to fail all of his own tests. He was re-slated to sit them again in September. Instead, he dropped out, never to return. Someone told Gavin that Jimmy had found a job in a warehouse, back home, packing and distributing books world-wide. He'd been reconciled with his wife.

Gavin had a last Christmas card from Jimmy. It said, "Keep playing, butt!" But he never did. In his second year he gave up Classical Studies for International Law. His parents were pleased.

The Bailey Report

"Here he comes," said Geraint Owen, the sound engineer, to his cameraman.

"At last," said Mickey Britt. "Stand by for irruptions, and assorted earthquakes, Ger."

The two men were dressed for the weather, any weather, in Corporation issue black anoraks and wide waterproof trousers. They were dressed for waiting. They both looked down the funnel of the terraced street, houses on each side for almost half a mile and cars parked nose-to-tail, to where the street sloping down to the valley bottom abutted onto the main road. At the junction, where only double-yellow lines were free of vehicles, the car they recognised as his had stopped, and parked on the double-yellow lines. It was a silvery blue Bentley, a coupé, with amber tinted windows and low-slung doors which closed with an assuring clunk when he stepped onto the pavement and shut the one on the driver's side. Right hand over left shoulder, without looking, he locked the car electronically.

A.J. Bailey was a man in late middle age. He had the broad, but loosely-held, shoulders of a middleweight boxer and the heavy legs of an Olympic oarsman, so he appeared to be longer above his tapered waist than below it. The late November morning was dank, edged with a coldness seeping down from the hills into the streets, but he wore neither overcoat nor raincoat, and no Corporation anorak, against the chill, only a bespoke single-breasted suit of grey worsted over a cobalt blue shirt with a button-down collar left open at the neck. As he strode up the street toward the waiting team he ran a comb through his thinning sandy-coloured hair, and he whistled, rather tunelessly, to himself.

At the far end of the long street, Donald Thomas, executive producer, sprawled across the back seat of a leased Corporation Volvo saloon. It was a diesel model, painted in Forest Green and with brown leather seats to match a walnut dash. The car came in the middle range of hired vehicles deemed suitable for someone at executive producer level. Donald Thomas curdled with resentment at the car's silent signifying of his rank. He hated what it registered, that he was nearer sixty than fifty, and that this was it for him. He had his eyes closed as he sat and waited in the car. He drummed his fingers against the headrest.

From the front seat of the Volvo, May Onions, his PA for over a quarter century, had been keeping watch. She half-turned to the back, "He's here, Donald," before staring back down the street past the patient, immobile Geraint Owen and Mickey Britt. In the Volvo, Donald Thomas opened his eyes, but only to glare at the back of the seat in front of him. "Oh, he is, is he? At fucking long last… at fucking long last… as fucking usual." Then, with a wrench of the handle, he opened the rear left-hand door of the Volvo and pulled himself up, and into the street. After the warmth of the car he shivered in the outside air and buttoned over a heavy cable knit sweater his fur-lined suede coat around his stomach. Not much of a belly, he felt, given his height, almost six foot, but maybe, he'd decided, enough of a belly to drive him to a gym someday soon. He ran a hand through the muss of back curls, with only a hint of becoming grey around the temples, and rubbed his prominent nose between finger and thumb. The twat, he thought. He stood stock still, as his presenter approached with a studied nonchalance, an insolent ease, which Donald Thomas hated even more than he disliked the Volvo the Corporation had bestowed upon him.

The late arrival waved at the crew of cameraman and sound recordist as he drew near, and blew a kiss, one made somehow into a lascivious gesture by sliding it off the palm of his turned over hand with a puff of his breath, to May Onions. She sucked on her lower lip and turned her back on him as she reached for a clipboard of notes in the car. May wore a woollen black bobble-hat over her auburn hair and a shiny black coat of stitched panels over blue jeans and suede ankle boots, so that she was, apart from a freckled face and sage-green eyes, quite covered up. The presenter smiled. He swivelled to greet his producer.

"Morning, Colonel," he said. "Are we set? Best get cracking, eh?" and, infuriatingly, he treated the annoyed recipient of his off-hand delivery to a lop-sided grin which was not contemptuous at all, no need for that, just intentionally dyspeptic in its effect. On Donald Thomas, that is. No apologies, and absolutely no explanation, for this, after all, was Bailey, and Donald Thomas knew in an instant, as he had been forced to know it many times before, that his anger, without any real means of redress, would be futile, and that even reasonable complaint, albeit merely verbal, would be self-defeating in the face of the tantrum it would undoubtedly cause. So, he just grunted, in a mutter of an aside, "For fuck's sake, Bailey," and gestured vaguely to the patient, indifferent crew who had balanced their Styrofoam coffee containers on the bonnet of their white Ford Estate car, and were waiting for the action to begin.

Bailey strolled across the street to talk with Mickey Britt. In the recent past the cameraman would have had an assistant to lug the gear, to set up the camera and even to pull the focus for the shot, but no longer. Nor was there a lighting man with his array of blondes and brunettes and redheads, the aptly named devices, to derive or deny tint and colour from the glare or dimness of the natural light. Nowadays there was only the camera, its reduced operator, and a soundman to mike-up or point the muffled microphone to the talking head. Bailey often reflected on the incremental disappearance of the latter, of people like himself, from documentaries and factual programmes. Yet, thank God! he would add, not from the gritty nit-picking of the investigative reports in which he had long specialised. His gift, so to speak, and, he'd conclude looking at the accumulating pension pot any freelance was required to feed, the gift that kept giving… for a while yet anyway. He suddenly felt, and looked, genial.

"Where do'you want me, Michael, me old mucker?" asked Bailey of his cameraman, and both nodded at each other in the shared recognition that any star presenter knew with whom his best interests rested. And it was certainly not with any producer.

Mickey Britt gestured towards the backdrop behind them where the sloping street began to climb further upwards to the mountain which was more of a protuberance than a peak. It was one of those squat, rounded hills of bracken and boulders which clamped a sullen presence over all the vistas to be glimpsed from the valley's floor of road, rail and river. To the left of the hill where it abruptly fell away and flattened out as if a shovel had cut into it was what they had come to investigate, or rather to show since the actual investigation, researched by May Onions and scripted by Donald Thomas, would be revealed by the footage Mickey Britt had already taken for Bailey's final voice-over in studio. What they were about "in situ" was precisely that: to add the authenticating touch of actual presence and perceived involvement – the Bailey trademark.

In the near distance, through the camera's viewfinder, men in yellow slipover jackets, and all with white or orange hard hats on, could be seen moving around the site. The soft thrum of dumper trucks mingled with the harsher revving of lorries in a suspension of whiteness, a dust flurry which never settled but floated amongst and beyond the encircling iron railings and open gates. This, in plain view, was the Mynydd y Caws waste disposal site, an open refuse disposal unit, set down on the cleared ground of a closed colliery's former tip. That signifying pyramid of coal, once teetering to an insolent height over houses and a school, had been levelled and grassed over after the Aberfan disaster of 1966. But the debris of industrial waste, just like the waste which had once spewed over these valleys, was still being re-cycled here for use elsewhere. If Bailey did irony he could have joined up the dots. Only Bailey did not do irony. Nor did he have any discernible political allegiance, not even cynicism or compassion. In life this made him, for those who did, like Donald Thomas, almost insupportable. On the box, however, it made for a strength of conviction that had all the direct simplicity of the best acting.

"We'll use that behind you, Bill," Mickey Britt told him. "You can assume it, there, over your right hand shoulder. It'll be in sight all the time… for the viewers…great picture, Bill."

Bailey allowed the liberty with his name. Some could, and some could not. For Mickey Britt, fellow incomer two generations removed, and as monoglot English a Celt as Bailey himself, there was no problem. Anyone else, though, had better know Arthur Joseph Bailey as "Mister Bailey" or call him "A.J.", or, better still, just "Bailey" if they knew what was both good for them, and appropriate for him.

Donald Thomas had stood off to one side. He ambled forward in a proprietorial shuffle and with a self-announcing cough. He looked through the viewfinder as if his opinion of the shot was the one, in the first and last resort, which mattered. Bailey had already moved centre frame. Donald Thomas jiggled his bent-over head in approval. Mickey Britt took a final look-see, and gave Bailey the thumbs-up. Donald Thomas moved between Bailey and the camera. He held out his hand. May Onions hurried forward with a script. To check… to be certain… ins and outs… for continuity. He conferred with Bailey who simply shrugged. Geraint Owen confirmed there were: no aeroplanes, no cars, no vacuum cleaners, no music, no troublesome kids, no rowing households: only the ambient buzz of traffic and industry and a soughing wind off a bedraggled copse on the otherwise bare bones of the hill. Perfect.

"Right," said Donald Thomas. "A run-through?"

"No," said Bailey. "Come on. Let's just go for it."

Mickey Britt chortled, and looked up at his producer, and then slyly at Bailey. "One Take Bill" was what camera crews had gratefully christened him. He never "corpsed" with the private, inexplicable inner glee at the absurdity of his role; he never fluffed a line or suffered sudden memory loss; he never tried to better what he'd already accomplished the first time. All this, over many years, had been a constant source of friction with his various producers who remained determined on the self-justification of having various takes from various angles: "For choice in the cutting room. Just in case. You never know. In the final edit."

So far as Bailey was concerned such professional belt-and-braces trainee school stuff was a waste of time, his time, valuable time when money at business conferences and government seminars and training videos was begging to be made elsewhere. This time, Donald Thomas didn't bother to argue the toss with the insufferable Bailey. He would get Mickey Britt to do some hand-held GVs later, for mood and for ease of editing, but for now all there was to do was to mutter, "Yeah. Go for it then. Ready, Mickey? Geraint? Right. Camera rolling."

Bailey rocked slightly on the balls of his Gucci-shod feet. It pulled him, almost imperceptibly, into the camera's lens. His face was immobile and his light blue eyes seemed transfixed for the heartbeat or two in which he said nothing. Then he half-rotated his upper body, but without ever taking his eyes off the camera, to suggest the presence of the Thing behind him. His voice when it finally came out of the silence he had created for himself, was in a resonant, rumbling, button-holing conversational tone. This was to be the opening of the programme. It was to be a signature Bailey piece-to-camera.

"Look… there… behind me. Would *you* like it behind *you*? Behind *your* street? Looming above the rooftops of *your* houses? Lurking in the air above the fields where *your* children are at play? Would you? I know *I* wouldn't.

But that's where *they've* put it, though, this *Thing*.

That's where *their* Council has put it. A State-of-the-Art refuse site, *they* say. The Mynydd y Caws Dump. And I say Dump, because that's what they do, that's where they dump, on open ground, close to these streets, not just household waste but untreated building materials, plastics, chemical matter, toxic stuff some say, biological and pharmaceutical discards.

And I'll tell you this, as I stand here in this street on this workaday morning, it's noisy, its filth is in the air, and it stinks in my nostrils. And the good people of these streets have to listen to the *Thing*, see the *Thing*, smell the *Thing* and breathe in its noxious fumes, day by day and night after night."

Bailey adjusted his stance and took a pace nearer the camera. He gave the camera a wry smile, an over-the-garden-wall confidence: "*They*... the Council... *They* say it's all within acceptable limits for legal emissions. They say it's not a health risk, or indeed any kind of hazard to public health. It's safe. It's necessary. It's well-managed."

His smile became a grim memory in an instant.

"*They*...the People who live here, who *have* to live here, say the *Thing*, that *Thing* behind me, has caused birth defects, chest problems, stinging eyes, sore throats, premature deaths of the young, and of the old, and a terrible psychological blight on all the lives of those who have no choice but to live here." He paused. The tone was level once more. "Who's right? And who's wrong?"

Bailey let the silence wrap itself around him. He looked deep into the camera. His knife-edge of a mouth widened to a resolute crease, and he said: "Well, there's only one way to find out, isn't there?" He turned his back to the camera and walked with a slow, purposeful step up the slope of the long terraced street towards the mountain and its tumorous waste tip. After no more than fifty yards, he pivoted on his heel and lengthened his stride until he was almost back to his starting point.

"OK, Squire? You get all that?" he shouted out as he walked, but not to his Producer, only to the cameraman who, again, gave him his customary thumbs-up signal. Donald Thomas gnawed at the sore spot on his bottom lip. He waited for Bailey to be within earshot for a whisper.

"Fine… fine… though you missed out on the health statistics we discussed, and the reasons for its being there in the first place, and such stuff. So we'll need to pick that up later, in studio, won't we? One way or the other. But since we were so late in starting, we'd better break now, hadn't we? For an hour. Be back, at the gates, while it's still light."

This last was mostly for May Onions who looked down at her clipboard and then, in a voice louder than Donald Thomas' musings, told everyone that there was a chippie on the main road or an Italian for frothy coffee and corned beef pasties, if they preferred, and outside the gates to the dump in an hour then, at one-thirty, OK?

Mickey Britt and his sound engineer began to pack up their equipment into the back of their car. They would drive it wherever they were going, no matter how near or far it was, and park it in full sight to foil the "thieving bastards round here". And everywhere else they ever went. May Onions glanced at Bailey, trying to gauge his mood, and assess his needs now that Donald Thomas had exerted a producer's timetable control. But Bailey said nothing and did nothing, other than to give them a perfunctory nod. He jangled his keys in his trouser pocket as he walked away from his colleagues. He zapped open the Bentley, slid into the driver's seat and turned the car around in a tight circle before accelerating away onto the main road where a passing van had to brake and sound its ignored horn.

"The bugger", Donald Thomas said. "The bloody, arrogant, self-centred sod… the bastard."

May Onions saw his point. She had acknowledged it for herself some time ago. No point in going there, though, she thought. She enquired instead, "Coffee, Donald? Join the Boys?"

"Sod that," said Donald Thomas. "And sod him, too. Come on, there must be a pub around here. I need a bloody drink."

* * * * *

Donald Thomas fished out a twenty pound note from his wallet and asked May Onions to "get the drinks in" whilst he "paid a visit". His PA took the money and pulled a face behind his retreating back.

"I expect that includes you, boys. Mickey, what's yours? And Geraint?"

Drinks were ordered, and fetched to their adjacent but separate tables. A large whisky and soda for Donald; pints of lager for the boys; and a lime-and-soda with ice for May. Home-cooked ham and chips to follow for the boys, with ham rolls for her and Donald.

Donald Thomas returned and sat, in a glum contemplation, slightly to one side of their table. It was warm, a steamy iron radiator heat, in the back bar of the cavernous red-brick Victorian pub which they'd found in the town. He took off his sheepskin coat and threw it over the back of a Windsor chair. It fell to the floor. May Onions retrieved it. She hung it up on a peg. She gave him his change. She sat down and waited for the mood music to begin. She knew it would. Donald Thomas always simmered before he boiled over. The crew were quietly sipping their drinks and tucking in. She nibbled at a chip. She waited. Donald Thomas had not touched his drink or his food. Instead he stared, as in a trance, at the cone of weak sunlight which was being beamed through a blue-and-red lozenge of a stained glass window so that it funnelled through the air a mote of dust which flickered, particle by particle, in a whirling suspense.

Donald Thomas was not actually thinking. He was free falling. Into his own past. A past that had once been so full of promise. Like himself. Into the present he tumbled. So unfulfilling. Like his unfulfilled self. Was it his fault? He couldn't see why. He still "had it all", as a former Controller had told him, back then at the beginning, and indeed thereafter as he occasionally inched his way without real conviction or desire, up to the famed Third Floor, but where he never secured a foothold beyond being there "in an acting capacity". His telegenic looks – the phrase used in the 1960s for being conventionally handsome – had weathered but had not deserted him. Some had even thought his brooding eyes and sensual lower lip had a touch of Richard Burton about them. It was the same lip he was biting now. And, he thought as he bit it, he'd had a proper degree at Oxford, not like Burton's wartime dalliance there but a 2nd Class in PPE at Jesus. The Welsh College, as it was known, despite the fact that its Welsh intake was in a minority even then. Still, lifetime connections could be, and were, made amongst those who would, chrysalis-like, turn into the professionals which a Welsh secondary education, whether good Grammar or minor public schools, intended for their academic caterpillars: barristers and solicitors, civil servants and professors, executives and diplomats, administrators and managers. Playing rugby football was not, of course, compulsory but it had added a sheen to the polish to be brought to becoming a "Professional Welshman"; and he'd been good enough, once or twice, to play not just for his College as a loose wing-forward but also for the university Seconds, the "Greyhounds". College societies allowed him to brush up on the hesitant Welsh of his boyhood, the tongue his solicitor father and housewife mother had scarcely used at home between themselves, or in the family at all, in the City in which, as with so many post-war contemporaries, they had settled after their own college education. Donald was to be set on an even more upward social path. Paths to be trodden carefully and gratefully in exactly the way of others like him before him. Yet by the Sixties, more enticing opportunities, particularly for those of his generation and upbringing, were accruing almost daily in a country busily creating a living, for some at least, out of itself as a cultural artefact. There were new highways that could as easily to be taken to public prominence, the fame that whispered of fortune, as any of the more traditional routes to security and comfort. If he had made a mistake at all in the early days of his broadcasting career, it was only perhaps in scorning the steady labour, and subsequent rewards, of the offered management training courses. He was, so many sirens assured him, with his looks, his intellect, his charm, his sonorous speaking voice, his quintessence of being a modern man in a Welsh idiom, a star-in-the-making. And from the off he had loved the attention he had been able to gather for himself by being, however instantly or briefly, at the centre of the moment, those moments only radio and television could conjure. He was a Presenter. He was a Personality. He was a Face. He Voiced Over. He read the News. He chaired and he interviewed. What he never became, as if there was an ingredient missing in his make-up, was a Broadcaster.

Donald Thomas, sometimes despite himself, knew exactly what that meant. That there was a disjunction between the ornament he was and the function to which he aspired. That, unlike other professions with their guarded and self-sustaining worlds, the true Broadcaster had to both reach out to and yet reflect the audience. But most of that audience was indeed other. His colleagues, sensing this, and besides, not possessing his other attributes, readily took to those roles behind the camera, and so away from its relentless gaze, which higher executive positions or strategic production thinking could, along with higher salaries, bring them. He bridled at the tedium of committees and baulked at the even temper required for management team work, notwithstanding the compensation available in the darker enjoyment to be derived from the backstabbing of Corporation politicking and the arse-licking of superiors. He clung, for far too long, to his original, narcissistic dream.

Over the decades Donald Thomas, stalwart and veteran, was increasingly channelled as a presenter into those adjunct programmes and early evening series whose softness and cheapness could accommodate his now less than compelling presence. Worse, when he complained that such output only buttressed or perhaps occasionally heralded the changes shattering their accustomed world – the pit and steel closures, the destruction of established ways of life, the uncertainties of politics, from left to right, the uneasy rhetoric of a nation revived, former class divisions papered over – then, on the Third Floor, wise heads nodded and decided to find a way to use his talents, to note his desire and placate his ego. He was, all said and done, one of their own. They made him a producer... a senior producer... an executive producer... a producer by any other name for all that.

Donald Thomas was to be involved, as he had wished, in the big events, the big issues, the pressing matters, the State of the Nation debates, in all of the glamour and gravitas which the Corporation hoarded as the rightful cultural capital of the nation's broadcaster. He worked hard to shape and direct these productions so that they might, in their turn, affect that culture. His ambition was no less than that. Yet, ruefully, and even as he chopped off as many of the Talking Heads of others that he could manage, he was inwardly confronted by the stubborn, deep and instinctive knowledge that though he had failed himself to be that automatic and personal connection between lens and living room, he had need of that power wherever its detestable source lay.

* * * * *

Bailey...Bailey...Bailey... the surname beat a persistent tattoo inside Donald Thomas' head. He reached over to pick up his drink. Bailey. He gulped down some of the whisky and soda, snorting as the bubbles darted up his nose. Bailey. They always turned to Bailey. Whose principal concern, the producer so often lamented to those above him on the Third Floor, was only money, the fee, the dosh, spondoolicks, the loot, pounds, shillings and no fucking pence in the presenter's own re-iterated mantra of demand. Bailey. Donald Thomas, whose own name credit-ended every decent programme Bailey had ever made let out an involuntary sigh.

How much he, Bailey, lacked. How much he, Bailey, seemed oblivious to all around him. Did he even know that, out of his hearing, for his temper was as ferocious as his fists were quick, they called him "Billy Boy"? Like a chirping budgie with an appetite for seed and an ever-open beak. Once a secretary, star-struck maybe, had sung "Bewitched, Bothered and Bewildered" at a Christmas Do and dedicated it to her "Pal Billy". Bailey had applauded her "lovely singing voice". Someone had once christened him "King Arthur" in ironic tribute to the discrepancy between Bailey's day-to-day behaviour and the regal flaunt of his TV persona. He seemed aloof, disinterested, untouchable. And then the green light went on and he was none of these things.

Donald Thomas said to May Onions as if she'd been sharing his thoughts all along, "The thing is, May love, the tosser is such, such…", and he paused to let the exact and appropriate word arrive from his Oxonian hinterland, "such a boor!". It was as if he'd had a sudden revelation ,or a returning one anyway: "He's boor-ish, so ipso facto, he's a boor."

May Onions remained silent. She was not, herself, quite clear how Bailey was a boor, or what the category of boorishness fully implied. She wondered if it was a categorisation people like Donald Thomas invented, required even, to denote people like Bailey. To distinguish themselves from those others who were not, ever, capable of being like them. Donald Thomas was unaware of her lack of certainty. His own absolute conviction was now both infinite and specific.

He sipped at his double whisky. His reverie returned. Time was when, at the start of their careers, he'd tried to be sociable with Bailey. Never, even in those days, Arthur or Joseph days, certainly not "Bill", and "A.J." sounded too boardroom, so it was always to be "Bailey", and no closer than that for Donald Thomas. He invited Bailey, and his wife – Rita, a nurse he recalled – to his house. His own wife, Nerys, had taken a day off school to prepare the dinner. None of that sickly pink prawn cocktail and glutinous boeuf bourguignon stuff which the world and his wife were dishing up at that time, usually to be followed by a crème caramel and the blue stilton with dimpled crackers. They were to have something to which the palate needed to pay attention. Something, for that time, exotically different. When the "Sopa fría de Ajo y Almendras con Uvas" appeared in its crock of white china, Bailey's eyes had directed his nose to sniff. At the first spoonful of the thick, white, bread-soaked liquid of ground almonds, water and garlic – almost a perfect replica of the deliciously refreshing soup Donald and Nerys Thomas had tasted in the hills of Andalucia the previous summer – Bailey ran his tongue over his lips and glanced up first at the dutifully slurping Rita, and then at his hosts.

"Supposed to be cold, is it? Only asking, my old flower, but I've got a grape in mine, too. Afters first, is it?"

He had spooned up half a bowl and declared himself to be "full as a tick" and "ready for mains". In those days the great oenophile had not achieved his transubstantiation out of the form of the beer-swilling Bailey, but he smacked down a glass or two of good claret with a hint of the wine bibbing future he might yet care to embrace. A platter of rice and pine nuts dotted with minced lamb meatballs and a layer of sticky brown dates and gooey orange quinces steamed onto the table in an aroma of sweet fried onions, and with the subtle herbaceous hints of Middle Eastern spices. "Oh, good," said Bailey, "Main meal and pudding in one. We'll get home early, Rita." The invitation was never reciprocated and, so far as Donald Thomas could recall, he never set eyes on the wife of the surprisingly uxorious Bailey again, though from time to time there was abrupt news of children being born whilst he and Nerys, her choice more than his, kept their parallel careers on track, and the lives of the executive producer and the headmistress of a primary school in the city proceeded in agreeable, childless fashion.

Donald Thomas chewed it all over again.

"You see, May," he said. "Someone like me looks at a Bailey and, well, should, in some ways, admire him. And why not? He didn't go to a particularly good school, one of the second-rate grammars in the city, and he didn't have the advantage of an Oxbridge education. Not even a university one... the local poly in fact... some kind of Mickey Mouse law and accountancy course. He never practised either. A stint in the Army hoping for a commission, but he gave that up to marry. Pregnant, probably, knowing him. Straight into local news reporting and then broadcasting... despite having no Welsh... not even passable Welsh, like mine was then... so, yes, of course, to be admired." Donald Thomas drained his glass. "But then why, oh why, is he so bloody obnoxious?"

It was not, of course, a question. Not one of any kind. In any case, May Onions had no answers to questions she would never have posed to herself in that or any such way. For her, Bailey was a phenomenon, a force of nature even, difficult and undeniably unpleasant when he chose to be, but, as she also felt, utterly distinctive, to the point of being unstoppable, whereas Donald Thomas was, well, nice enough, self-deprecating, charming when he stopped whining, but self-absorbed where Bailey was self-directional. She had been sucking up her pale green lime-and-soda drink through a colourless plastic straw. She finished when the sump at the bottom of the glass filled with air and made its slightly farty sound in the mouth at the final suck. Donald Thomas had not stopped talking – to himself of course – so she tuned in again.

"And what's all that Army stuff all the time with him? Where does that all come from? He was only there long enough for basic bloody training. I'll tell you why... cos he's a snob underneath it all, underneath all that weepy stuff about council houses, an abusive, alcoholic and then absent father, and a saintly mother out scrubbing floors for her Joseph. Onwards and upwards for him. He *loved* swanning around an Officers' Mess, I bet... losing his twang quicker than he could wink. I bet he sucked up there. Colonel! Major! Captain! Sergeant-Major! General! My arse.

"Let's face it…we put up with him but for how much longer? He's insufferable…Tony Hancock on speed! Decades out of date and snide to boot."

Donald Thomas needed rescuing. They could all feel it. May Onions didn't know where to start. Mickey Britt was pensive. He'd heard the diatribe, in one of its many forms, and more than once, from his nominal boss. Since Bailey and he were akin in their upbringing so far as working-class parents of second generation Brummie origin went, and with a disciplining, yet socially limiting, education to match, he could himself understand and so excuse Bailey's mix of combative aggression and touchy sensibility… more readily, anyway, than Donald Thomas ever could. Mickey Britt even admired the brute manner in which Bailey had spurned the drummed in, leaden persistence of the know-your-place education which they had had in common. Bill Bailey, Mickey Britt knew, was no gent, and never would be. Donald Thomas, though, personified the caste, at least in its local guise, and was always courteous to his staff colleagues. As a mark of respect for the issue before them, an attempt at reassurance for Donald Thomas, in a gesture of almost professional solidarity, Mickey Britt tried to help with a definition of his own, one closer to home.

"Yeah, Don," he said, his own original inner city vowels as sharply defined and slicing in intonation as ever, "proper old fuckin' ba-a sta-ard when he wants, inne?

Donald Thomas coughed in disdain at the distasteful language. May Onions flashed Mickey Britt the chiding look of an intermediary smoothing matters over for the great and good. Geraint Owen, as he had learned to do since leaving the north for the south, kept his private thoughts close to himself. May Onions decided to intervene, but in a lesser, more amused vein of recollection.

"Then again, Donald, what about the time we were filming that Welsh-restaurant-in-the-Dordogne story, Michelin stars for Merthyrborn couple, and all that? Lovely meal, wasn't it? But A.J. so grumpy, and off to bed early, only the adjoining hotel I'd booked, corporation rates in play, wasn't to his liking, so he came back to the restaurant and I had to drive to that chateau on the edge of the town. Set in parkland… lovely… and charming English-speaking proprietor… nice-looking, too.

Anyway, our man barges up to reception and blurts to the young woman behind the desk, "Bonjour, my Cherie, chamber large, yes?" And the owner steps in and says he's had my call and reserved a special room for the "Famous Corporation" and before he can finish, speaking perfect English, mind, Bailey jumps in and says, "Splendido, my frère. But, listen, this is just for moi, see, so ensure, comprendee? that it's a Grand Chamber with private sale-de-bain. Gracias mucho, count." The Marquis, I'm sure he was, looked as if a dog had vomited all over his Aubusson. That's a carpet, Mickey!"

Donald Thomas permitted himself a pouting smile.

"Yes, you told me over the cognac later. Embarrassing git… what he is, at heart, what he truly is, because I don't believe he doesn't know what he's up to, is… feral."

Mickey Britt had liked the modest French hotel May Onions had booked. But he had also seen the Dordogne chateau when they picked Bill up in the morning. He had waved from a sun-dappled terrace, the remnants of his breakfast of freshly squeezed orange juice, coffee, rolls and croissants, scattered in disarray before him, and the Marquis laughing with him, but in service at his side. Mickey Britt had sensed a flush of pride rising. One of our own. In the pub, now, he considered that "feral" was perhaps "Fair Do's", but that Bill Bailey was better understood as "fierce and fearless". Donald Thomas pushed his empty glass to the edge of the table. He watched Mickey Britt and Geraint Owen snaffle the untouched ham rolls. In the far corner of the echoing bar-room an old man left his high stool at the bar. He shuffled over to an old-fashioned juke-box set against the wall, inserted a coin and punched a button without looking. In a whoosh of slithering strings the chord-roasted tones of Nat King Cole swooped in and warmed the room:

> "Unforgettable, that's what you are
> Unforgettable though near or far
> Like a song of love that clings to me
> How the thought of you does things to me …"

"Oh, Christ!" said Donald Thomas. "That's the tin lid, that is. Come on, let's go."

* * * * *

Two o'clock outside the gates, Bailey had not appeared. The camera was already up on its tripod in a fixed position. To the north-west of the council refuse site the winter sun was fast sliding down the mountain ridge. Bailey refused to give his mobile number to anyone. Besides, it was permanently off, subject to his view that he used it to reach people when he wanted, not when they required him. In the back of the car Donald Thomas and May Onions sat in silence side by side. She wondered if she should pat his hand… or perhaps not.

Donald considered what he had heard other people in command call available "nuclear options"… an official complaint… a dressing down… an enquiry… a sacking… or perhaps not. He sighed.

May Onions looked again at her own option. His hand… then at her right, free hand. In her other hand, the left, she held her mobile. It buzzed and she grabbed it with the hand that had been momentarily free. She pressed Answer. It was Bailey.

"Hiya, love… A.J. here…been delayed… on the way, OK? Fifteen mins… see you babe."

"Well," said Donald Thomas. "Well? What excuse has the shit got this time?"

May Onions contemplated the moods to come. She rehearsed in her mind the tempers that would fray. She surveyed mentally the best outcome for the show. She acted in its best interests.

"It's his mother," she said.

"His mother? His fucking mother?" gasped Donald Thomas.

"Yes. I should've said earlier, Don, but he asked me not to. Was why he was late this morning, too. He said he didn't want to cancel or make a fuss. She fell in the night. She's in sheltered accommodation, you know. On her way to the loo. They only found her this morning. They called an ambulance. Hospital. It seems she's broken her hip. They, uh, after this morning's shoot, A.J., uh, belted back down the dual carriageway to see her. She'll have to have an op. She's about 96. Not his fault this time."

"He could have told me directly. I'd've postponed it. But that greedy bugger would've seen a loss of earnings elsewhere on his packed schedule!"

"He is close to her, you know, Donald. He was only eight when his father left."

"You swallow that d'you, May? The absconding pater familias, the old lady taking in washing and doing cleaning to keep Saint Bill in school? Jesus, May…"

"As a matter of fact, Donald, yes, I do," asserted May Onions. "And he just said he'd be breaking the speed limit to come and finish the prog, so give him a break, OK?"

Donald Thomas shook his bushy head from side to side. Incredulous, rather than denying her plea he slumped back into his seat. May tapped on the window. She gave Mickey Britt and Geraint Owen the ubiquitous thumbs up – waiting time over soon.

Inside the chain-link fence dumper trucks were using their shovels to cut avenues of access between the piled up refuse. Mickey Britt took a few more GVs without his producer needing to ask. The man who'd played Nat King Cole in the pub was clumping unsteadily up the steep dirt-track road to the site. He nodded to the camera more than to its operator and walked up to the Volvo where Donald Thomas, his eyes closed, still sat. He rapped hard on the window. May Onions put her chewed-up biro and clipboard down on the next seat and pressed the button to open the electric window on her side.

"Yes?" she said. "Can I help you?"

The man at the open window was in his late seventies. He wore a thin black mackintosh over a grey polo-neck jumper. He was unshaven, a grey stubble pocking his scrawny neck. His breath was a waft of inhaled, re-routed and exhaled untipped cigarettes and the woody, sweet afternote of draught bitter.

"Ay," he said. "Perhaps you can. They told me, back in the pub, that you're filmin' up 'ere 'bout that tip, and stuff. S'right?"

Donald Thomas had opened his eyes. He leaned slightly across his PA. In a protective manner, not sure where this was leading.

"You 'aven't got Council permission, 'ave you?" the old man said. "Permits 'n 'at."

Donald moved his hand closer to the window. "Hang on mate," he said. "Hang on. That's not entirely fair, you know. And, besides, I think you'll find we're here to help."

"Help? Help? You're jokin' are you?" said the man. "Don't talk to me 'bout help. This will be another side show, a circus, a news story. A joke."

In the distance, beyond the old man's grizzled head, Donald Thomas could see Bailey trudging up the road. The old man shifted his own stance to follow the producer's eye-line.

"Is that that Bailey, then?" he asked.

"Yes", said Donald Thomas wearily. "That is indeed that Bailey."

"Well, I'd bloody well like to have a word or two with him as well then, right?" growled the stranger. "He needs telling something he does, if he's with you, that is."

"Yes, fine," said Donald Thomas. "Fine. You give him, my friend, if

I may be so bold, the benefit of your considerable experience, and clearly your correct and entitled opinion. Go ahead. Be my guest. Just give it to him… preferably with both barrels."

Bailey was yelling, "Sorry, Boys" as he approached the camera position. He offered May Onions a hand wave as thanks. May Onions scrambled out of the car. She said, loudly, enough to be heard, "Sorry to hear about your mum's fall, A.J… hope she'll be all right." Bailey made a puzzled frown. "Eh?" he said and then, recovering, "Yes. Ta, she's OK, I think. Last time I looked anyway." Then he almost bumped into Donald Thomas and the producer's new-found friend, both standing in the road and in his way so that Bailey said, genially enough for him, "Move over, chaps… we've got to do this pretty quick, eh… before the light goes. All in my head, Donnie, no worries… don't you fret… here I am… will be word-perfect… as agreed… just for you, mon General."

The old man did not move. He jabbed out a nicotine stained finger at Bailey. The distended knuckle wobbled as he waggled it in Baileys's blank face.

"I've been wanting to meet you for years, I 'ave."

"Really?" said Bailey. Why's that then, Tosh?"

"I'll tell you why," said the old man, and he wiped a work-swollen hand across the spittle of his lips.

"I'll tell you why," he repeated as Bailey waited.

"With all we have to put up with… patronising buggers coming up 'ere when it suits… and only then. Patronising buggers, like your lot, coming up 'ere, as if from another planet, takin' your bloody pictures, makin' us all out to be 'opeless, dim-witted, doo-lally-tap, 'elpless left-overs, relics. As if we 'ad nothin', done nothin', 'ad no history to speak of, just remnants, to be sorry for. No idea most of the time of who we were, leave alone what we are now. What we actually may still be, 'cos there's no clue in their 'eads, is there, of what might be in our 'eads, that we might be thinking, behind the closed doors of those 'ouses none of them ever thinks to enter and ask, when the curtains are drawn and we're not being given parts to play, uh?"

The old man was shaking. He seemed to have run out of breath. Bailey set his lower lip into a Bailey jut.

"And your point is, soldier?" he said.

"My point is, Mister Bailey," said the old man, "is that you, and I'd say only you, seem to understand the half of what I've just told you. I dunno much about you, but I've seen you giving those buggers set above us, by themselves most of the time, an 'ard time, whoever they are. I know you're not from 'ere, not one of us, directly like, but you can't 'elp yourself can you? From being with us, as well, to expose them, to chivvy the buggers, beat 'em up when they don't answer the questions they don't want to hear, and which you still ask. And, if you 'ave to, bring the fuckers down, uh?"

"Right-o," said Bailey. "Couldn't have put it better myself, could I Donald? Now, if it's OK with you, Sunny Jim, I've what we in the business call A Piece to Camera to do. Stay and watch if you like. But behind the camera, please."

Bailey shook an outstretched hand. He walked past the old man. He winked at a crestfallen Donald Thomas. Mickey Britt pointed to his marked position, and asked, "What the fuck was that all about?" Bailey took up his position in front of the camera. He said, quietly enough, "Fuck knows, Michael, some local paysan Donnie boy picked up. Shall we do this, then? Get it over with? I've got something on in town at five o'clock, got to change first."

Bailey's face was suddenly shadowed into seriousness by some inner mechanism he controlled when he needed it. Mickey Britt checked, and approved, the light. It was just sufficient, a glimmer which penetrated the whole and made a chiaroscuro cameo from which Bailey could shine out. Geraint Owen asked for a sound check. Bailey said, "Tiddley Tum, Tiddley Tum, what's the price of a sack of coal nowadays. Down the hatch." Mickey Britt respectfully raised an eyebrow for Donald Thomas to start proceedings officially, but the producer was gazing into another space and it was May Onions who said, "Go for it, then A.J.."

Bailey had not lost his concentration. He moved, but again only fractionally, to animate his stance, and he began, and ended, in one take.

"Here in this valley, indeed in all our industrial valleys, there have lived people of quality. Vintage communities, created out of appalling conditions, by the people themselves. Self-confident people, proud people, whose very existence has shaped our history, yes, the history of all our nation, like no other force in the past one hundred years. They deserve, in these latter days, better than this. To be dumped upon. Like this... thing behind me. You know, I have concluded that this is not a question of who's right and who's wrong, of statistics or efficiency savings, of managerial capability or scientific expertise. It is, quite simply, a question of common humanity, and of our duty, all of us, to that humanity, as it exists, on the ground, here. On *their* front doorsteps... in *our* backyard. There is only one feasible conclusion to draw from our investigation in this programme. That Thing over there should be stopped. It will be stopped. It must be stopped. To let all who live here, who choose to live here, who have the right to live here, listen again to birdsong not diesel engines, to breathe fresh air not noxious fumes, to smell spring on the mountains, not scent death in their valleys."

Bailey counted one-two-three to himself. He shifted his head, so that his eyes seemed to glitter with a new force.

"This programme has been, as always, a calling card on behalf of the people who matter. You. I'm A.J. Bailey, and you've been watching the Bailey Report. Thank you and, until next time, goodnight."

* * * * *

Donald Thomas thought: "Christ… he thinks he's a bloody American." May Onions decided it was "cheesy", even for A.J. Mickey Britt confirmed it was "a wrap". Geraint Owen wandered off to record "some wild track". The old man applauded, and slapped Bailey on the back as the presenter strode past him. Bailey, without looking back, waved a hand at them all as he left the scene.

Counteractual

The old man watched Bailey retreat down the street. He saw Pigeon slide off the low cream-coloured concrete window sill of a garishly painted terraced house. Bubble-gum pink for the walls and baby blue for the woodwork. He saw Pigeon flip a half-smoked cigarette in Bailey's direction and wave him away with a vigorously waggled V-sign and a muttered, "Piss-off outahere."

He waited for Pigeon to turn on his heel to walk towards him. The old man looked past Pigeon to check that Bailey had reached his car. He had. He had paid Pigeon no attention. The car, with the TV Presenter at the wheel, moved off in a hurry. The old man walked slowly towards Pigeon. When they stood face to face on the pavement in the middle of the street Pigeon looked down at the old man, ready for him to speak first. In the silence between them Pigeon was impatient. He shouted loud enough for an audience.

"Wassa 'bout butt? He's offa telly innee? a tossa there. 'Ee can fuck off forrastart, an all. Saaright, butt?"

The old man tilted his creased and pallid face up towards Pigeon, so closely that his stubble almost scratched the teenager's scrawny throat.

"Yes, he is," the old man said. "And there's no real requirement for you to speak like that now that he's gone and they've finished filming. And they are out of hearing so long as you desist from shouting."

"Sorry," said Pigeon. "It's just that I thought you'd said we had to keep it up… under all circumstances."

"Yes, by all and every means. But only when it is necessary for them. Not between ourselves, eh?"

Pigeon took off his NYC back-to-front baseball cap. He looked back up the street where the TV crew were packing up their gear.

"Are they really that thick?" he asked.

The old man sighed. "No, not thick exactly. Just a trifle obtuse, where other people are concerned. They can't read our signals so readily. We don't go around with coal-black faces anymore. Our politics no longer frightens them. We are no visible threat to their own conception of society, though that, of course, we hope, may change one day, again. You see, we are, in their eyes, poor. So we must be lesser. We stay here by choice, so we cannot be, oh, sacred word, aspirational. You can see why, then, it would not be helpful in the firmament of their fixed universe if we were to be discovered enjoying Beethoven, discussing Matisse's cut-outs, or reading Updike and Mailer. Or indeed, as you do yourself, be found grappling with Foucauldism as a metaphor for our auto-incarceration. We speak as we do before them only for them. It is necessary to sustain their illusion by deluding them."

Pigeon sighed in his turn. He sucked on his lower lip and gave the old man a petulant look, one that hinted at having heard something very similar from him a number of times. He decided to try another tack.

"I know it's a waiting game. I do know that. But what exactly, whilst we wait, do we get out of it?"

"Ah," said the old man to whom, over the years, this query had been put in the public, yet secret, meetings that had been held, in closed session, since the set-back of the Great Strike a quarter of a century earlier.

"What is at stake, my boy," he said, "is not what we currently get – the grants, the funding, subsidiarity, inward investment, regeneration projects, public works of art, entrepreneurial pods, electrification of the rail network, touring concerts and opera, visits from our national drama companies, and every other species of economic and cultural munificence we can garner – no, what is at stake is, first, why and how we get it. And the answer to that is by being, stubbornly, us and by staying, very much bloody minded, where we are. Think of it this way, too," he said. "Imagine if the Sioux had not gone, quietly in the end, with Red Cloud onto the reservation. Imagine if they had been able to stay out on the Great Plains with the resurgent spirit of Crazy Horse in their veins. Well, we have managed that, haven't we? Inside our own heads, I mean. Together, still, in ways they are not. Nor have ever been."

"But then?" said Pigeon. "After all this, then what?"

The old man clasped the young man around his shoulders. "The values which validate us, our past into our future through this present vale, cannot be allowed to shrivel up. To become, if you like, the clichés a Bailey will spin about us as tight-knit communities and the heart-warming victim syndrome. Because a pit closes, all of them in fact, or a factory closes, or even if a generation disappears like mine will soon, it does not mean that we cannot live as if the normal, our particular human contribution to history and morality, cannot be, for us, the norm."

Pigeon moved in step as the old man took his elbow and began guiding him back down the street.

"Look. Consider it this way," said the old man. "The more we are perceived as different, impossible cases perhaps, the more we will receive the benefits due to our being disabled from any utility in their utlitarian world. Best to let us fester outside their city – region. Keep us quiet, quiescent you might say. The danger is if they decide not to leave us alone, to wallow pityingly about our benighted condition. For then we might be sucked into their soul-less, deracinated lives of get-and-go, into their look-alike pattern -book housing on their digitally-modelled estates, bombarded by their aimless electronic chatter, their faceless tweeting of trivia, their closed circuitry of surveillance and the overall tyranny of their de-humanising technological devices. If ever an Orwellian phrase was waiting to be coined in St. George's dystopian name it was, surely, Social Media. A-social. Antisocial. Code for cod. Sharing by pairing. Paring the possible to the bone for the boneheaded."

He stopped stock-still. A guru on his own patch. Not to be denied. Pigeon relaxed.

"If they think," the old man said with some force applied to the young man's arm, "If they think we cannot aspire to be them, prevented by our heritage, our genes, our tribalism, whatever, from being able to join them, then, with a brute equivalence of motive and silent condemnatory accusation, we must strive to ensure we do not, ever, sink below them. For that would be to drown in the shit of their making without even the compensation of being ourselves the defecators of such a tragic destiny as their's surely is. So, you see, we require a holding strategy, a defence against the Midwichery of their Moonie herd. For they are the real tribalists, not us, and our togetherness, at its collective best, has always been about full individual liberation not the falsity of having to choose from a prescribed set of options. They think, as they view our limitations, real enough I grant you, that we are the ones who are imprisoned. On the contrary, we are the ones who can be free in ways they will never, for themselves, comprehend. What, therefore, we do together, increasingly into the future and as consenting adults, of course, as citizens if you will, is something they can no longer do, and which they would prevent us from doing if they knew: to relate the one to the other, to cohere, to have common purpose for common wealth, to inherit who we were so that we may create who we wish to be, to survive as ourselves in order to live on, as ourselves, not to live, even well, just in order to exist."

Pigeon released his arm and elbow from the old man's grip, and rubbed them. "Mmmm," he said and stared into the distance. The sun had sunk even below the lowest of the darkened hills. The two walked in a slow lock-step towards the bus stop on the main road. Pigeon looked at his e-bay purchased wrist watch. A fiver. Brand guaranteed. He shook his wrist from side-to-side to start it up again. In the gathering gloom, they sheltered behind the cracked perspex shield of the bus-stop's canopy against the wind scurrying up the valley. The old man decided that to clinch the argument, for the present, he needed another example to illustrate the necessity of defence before attack.

"D'you remember," he reflected, "how we were almost caught out about a year ago? They'd come up, as usual, with their fold-away camera and hairy caterpillar mikes, to take some vox pop on the latest government announcement: What do the people here think – do they think is what they really mean – of the proposed shift to reduced and universal benefits? And what they wanted, so that neither they nor their viewers would themselves have to think, of course, was the usual know-nothing, chopsy, keeper of the slurred, glotally over-endowed and strictly incomprehensible local accent. Preferably a morbidly obese, blowsy woman in her late thirties, with a fag in one hand, a can of extra-strength in the other, and an ignored baby crying in its pram. And, naturally, we were, as ever, prepared, on the look-out, ready, and able to station Tracy, after just twenty minutes in make-up in the Centre, right in their path. Irresistible. And she was."

"And we were rumbled?" asked Pigeon.

"Almost. Almost. Not quite. Tracy had been brilliant:

Lookewe. Owswegonna live, eh? Ows I gunna feed 'er? And she'd gestured with the cigarette in the direction of the child we'd borrowed and blew some smoke, not very much of course, towards the baby's face: *If ew sods or them sods takeawaysee, 'er rights, like, she'll starve to death, she will, 'onest. And I'm not 'avin aat ?, see. There'll be blood on the streets, innit? Like ah Miners' Strike all over again. Only worse, men'l see to aat, don't ew worry. Only worse. And , me personal like, I got a disability, aaan't I? And my old man's buggered off n'all, see. Some piece from Swansea.* At that, dear old Tracy burst into tears and put her pudgy hand to her lipsticked mouth as she bawled. They ate it up. Made all the news bulletins, Welsh and national UK."

The old man pursed his lips. The bus was swaying down the valley towards them. He tapped Pigeon on the arm.

"Only, the trouble was that the sound man had left his tape running for wildtrack nearby as he went off to help the cameraman load the car, and when he played it back he heard something, and we heard it clearly since Tracy and I, me in attendance naturally, had not moved: *My God. Did you see their scrunched-up, contemptible little faces. They really, truly, wanted me to be less than human, didn't they? So I gave them my best thespian works. But, you know, even then, in character, I was still human, wasn't I? Not in their prejudiced excuse for a life I wasn't. I was an oik. A scrounger. A nobody. A no-hoper. A scumbag. Well, scuttle back off to your sewer, you rats, and feed your transferred poison to your bosses. Me, I'm off to evening class at the Centre. Short stories from Chekov to Carver, without a Cartland in sight.*

We could see, immediately, the confusion it caused. The recording chap looked hard at Tracy. But the breeze and some sound from up the street had distorted it a bit. He was, in a sense, thank goodness, unwilling to believe what he'd actually heard. I sidled over as he re-played the wildtrack. I grinned at him. I said, 'Wassamarra, butt? Aaahs all come offa radio, mun. Schoolteachah biddy, uppa road, allus loppin' inna sum clever-dick play, or somepin, she is. Cow, mun.' I left it there. And so did they. Or else, I tell you, the game might have been up, and the first steps of revelation might have begun to suck us into their world of sensibility and submission."

Pigeon stuck out a hand to hail the bus. The driver took Pigeon's bus fare, gave out a ticket and waved the old man and Pigeon on and into the bus with a "Good afternoon, gentlemen". They sat, together, at the back as the bus crawled, stop by stop, filling up along the way, down the valley to the Heritage Park at the valley's mouth. Pigeon and the old man knew most of the faces on the bus. Nearly all were amongst the cast assembled locally for that night's performance. The first of the season in the Heritage Park's small theatre. The committee had decided to dramatise the Tynewydd Colliery mine rescue of 1879. Exploring underground flooded workings. Trapped man. Heroic rescue work. A boy scared. Medals for bravery bestowed. It was due to start, ninety minute tableau of dialogue and effects, rehearsed for weeks, at 7 o'clock that night. The first Cultural Tourism coaches from the Capital, generally genealogically-alerted Americans, would be arriving around six. Plenty of time, the old man said, to get into costume and to melt back into Victorian character. Then, by nine o'clock the cast would assemble again, with some invited others, in what they knew amongst themselves, as the Centre, to consider the lessons to be learned from further study of pre-1914 syndicalism in the Rhondda and workers' cooperatives in post-Independence Bengal. The old man would lead the discussion of the former and sit back to learn from their guest speaker's knowledge of the latter. They had all embraced the need for the long haul. Their retrieved culture would be ransacked to inform their future politics. But for now he leaned over to Pigeon, slipping in and out of the actual present to ready himself for a re-enactment of the past.

"Oi, butty," he said. "Tonight, mind, when it goes dark and you're supposed to be trapped when the workings flood, remember you, David Hughes, are only thirteen, and thinking you'll drown, and die, so remember to shake with fear, real fear, because it's actually happening. Only, me, Isaac Pride, master collier, risking life and limb to tunnel towards you after you've been trapped for four days, you and your butties, me, Isaac Pride, will take you and hold you tight in my arms so that you're to stop shaking and sobbing when I say, 'Now, now, boy bach. Now, now. We'll 'ave ewe back with ewer Mam in no time at all, butty. No time at all.'

"Orright, Grancha ," said Pigeon. "Orright. Only don't kiss me and squeeze me too tight, like you did in dress rehearsal, eh? Or else some of them punters might get the wrong impression. Innit, butt."

Avengers

Pitfalls

For him, killing them had always been easy. He was familiar with it. He even liked doing it. It was a release for him. The bludgeoning of them. A kicking. Punching. Strangling, Drowning them. Taking one of his sharpest knives, there were many, to cut their throats. The manner of it depended on his mood, and the circumstances they had caused. How he did it had never been a problem for him. Moving the bodies, to be rid of them, had become the problem. So the next one to transgress would be killed on the spot where the body would also disappear. It would need to be a bullet for it to be quick and easy. The one he called Nigger was the first one to be shot. He had left his teeth marks, white indents on her pink skin, punctuation points more than actual bites, on her freckled right forearm. That was enough for her grandfather. He told her so, and that it would happen as soon as he was ready. The girl had cried then, even tried to reason with him, that it was her own fault for encouraging him, by being so playful with him. Nothing she could say could move her grandfather. He'd made up his mind the moment he saw her arm. He had his rules. Few were ever able to keep them for long.

Two years before it had been Tiny who had to be punished. He was always hungry, mooching around the back kitchen door, for scraps of food. She let him come into the house though she knew the rules forbade it. But that was not what had caused him to be killed. He'd taken one of the chickens which were kept behind a wire mesh fence which penned them into their dirt-packed run in the back garden. In his hunger he must have sensed one would not be such a loss.

Her grandfather kept a dozen hens at a time, for eggs and, after he slaughtered them at Christmas time, for selling and eating. She used to watch him through the side kitchen window when the time came to kill them. He would fling six or seven birds at any one time into the flagstoned back yard. The chickens would open their wings. They would flutter and then cower into corners whilst he clutched them, one by one, and sliced their pre-historic heads off their jerky, feathered necks. She was fascinated by the blood which spurted from them in squirts of bright red string before falling onto the flagstones as bright globular bubbles, pooling wine-dark. She was always astonished, year by year, that the headless hens would continue to hop about, running and flapping their wings in one last attempt to fly off to a safer place. One by one, she knew, they would flop to the ground, fall onto the feather beds their frenzy had created and die in their own blood and shit. He would pick them up then and hang them upside down from the washing line to drain away their last flow of blood.

Tiny had been sated at last and dozing in the outhouse shed where he lived when her grandfather came across his dog, and the ripped yellow flesh and scavenged pink bones of the chicken carcase. His anger possessed him. He picked up the heavy shovel. He hit the sleeping Tiny with it, over and over, until the head was smashed and flattened into a pulp of blood and brain and bone. When dusk came he wrapped Tiny's bulk in sacking and put him in a wheelbarrow. When night fell he pushed the wheelbarrow down the back lane and across the field to take Tiny's corpse to the disused mine shaft which was now only used as the means of pulling fresh air into an adjacent pit workings as a downcast. Though he was wiry, he was not a big man or young anymore, so bumping the wheelbarrow and its inert load along an overgrown path in the woods which skirted the river, and then hauling the whole thing backwards across a mound of broken bricks and rubble tired him so that he cursed out loud. He threw the heavy body down the shaft to join the others he had variously dispatched and disposed of there in the past. But the effort was too much that time with Tiny, and he vowed he would never do it that way again.

Which is why he had decided, in advance, to deal in cold blood with any future breaker of his rules with a bullet. He could, he knew, buy a gun for a few quid and some consideration. Fresh meat he'd butchered, or maybe some of that old fashioned brawn his wife made for a special treat. It was the gun he'd seen, oiled and ready, unwrapped from its cotton covering beneath the table at the Legion Club. It was a Webley, a big heavy pistol for keeping British order overseas since Victoria was on the throne, and for close arms firing in both World Wars. This one was one of the latest models, purloined from an officer in the second, and last, of those wars. The one in which his son had died. There would be no questions asked. He arranged it within days of the latest transgression. It would be the way to do it from now on. With the gun, snug in his pocket after a session at the club, he decided they would walk together to the shaft. It would be easier, too, if he made the girl go with them. Besides, it would be a lesson for her as well. To see it happen. To realise why it was happening. So it wouldn't have to happen again. Perhaps.

He pulled her from her bed at two in the morning, and made her dress. They fetched the dog from the shed. He walked two paces behind her and, as he called him now, "Your Nigger". They stumbled through the undergrowth where the woods edged up to the riverbank. It was clammy in the late summer even at this time of the morning. She could smell the buttery rum on his breath in the stillness of the night. At the lip of the shaft he pushed them forward, together, so that they teetered on the very edge. The girl had said nothing. She felt fear, but uncertainty too as if the lesson which was being taught was not clear yet. He took the dog's rope lead from her hand and held it in his left. He pushed her to one side. Then she saw the heft of the long-barrelled pistol in his other hand, and when "her Nigger" turned his neck, straining to see her, he shot him between his deep black eyes. A third eye, a dark red hole of an eye, gaping and bleeding, sprouted between them. The girl screamed so he slapped her smartly across her cheek, and as she shook, gulping on her sobs, he toe-ended his latest victim, the first he had ever shot, into the void. The returning sound was a muffled whump from the long fall to the bottom of the shaft where the bones of the coal black terrier she had loved too much would rest with those of the too greedy bulldog. That night she, too, decided something. That she would hate her grandfather forever. Or, at least, until he died.

* * * * *

The terror through whose random application he ruled did not stop or start with animals. Domestic disobedience, however trivial or unintended, would have a violent outcome. When he returned from the trenches of the First World War in which as a sapper he had scuttled about like a rat, a collier rat, one amongst many so praised for their underground and undermining skills behind enemy lines, he was be-medalled and, they said, be-mused by shell shock into bursts of anger. His wife saw most of those bursts at first hand, and behind closed doors. He would bunch up his bony little fists and beat out a tattoo on her face and her shielding arms. For weeks at a time she would, after these assaults, not be seen outside the house. He would skulk in whichever Workmen's Club he was favouring at the time and sink into the oblivion of beer and whisky chasers. He was not alone in this, nor in his behaviour. His wife, though ever silent on the subject, had reasons of her own to know that it was not the war in itself, the cloak for his savagery, which had triggered his lifelong malevolence. As best she could she protected her son. Since poverty was everwhere in those years between the wars, their own condition of misery did not seem so exceptional. They survived on bits and pieces of war pension and dole money, and the work his wife did as a seamstress or washerwoman for others. When work increased at the pits with the approach of another war, it was the boy who did it, and brought his money home. The new war took him away, though not before he had married. His wife was pregnant with their child and working in a munitions factory when they received the telegram telling of his death at the beachhead at Anzio in Italy in 1944. It seemed another of the hammer blows of fate which none could escape at that time in that place. When their daughter was born the mother found work in a post-war brake-lining factory on the new Industrial Estate. Her wages were sunk into the household until, one day, she was no longer there, and none could find her. The child was, once more, kept from her grandfather's rages by the wife who had stayed through it all, until in the girl's tenth year her grandmother became bed-ridden with the slow cancerous growth which would, surely they all said, tut-tutting on visits to the kitchen and bearing home-cooked pies and stews for the stricken family, kill her. He said, furious at the smell of sickness in the bedroom, that the famous White Medicine, which hung in gloopy suspension in its oversize bottle like a milky concentration of spermatozoa, would likely do the trick by itself.

It was the girl, more absent than not from school, who tended to her grandmother and turned to serve his needs by washing, ironing and mending his faded and patched clothes. Nothing had ever been shop-bought in that house, so she had learned from her grandmother how to bake bread, make a thin stew of root vegetables and cheap cuts of meat, how to strain and re-use tea leaves and water the milk, and fry the occasional rashers of bacon he brought home when flushed with his winnings on the horses. He worked on his allotment, near the river, and from it, grown and harvested seasonally, would come potatoes and onions, radishes and tomatoes, runner beans and peas, carrots and leeks, and sweet strawberries which he would generously give to neighbours who would then think him not so bad as some made out.

The chickens were fed from troughs of grain in their wire-fenced run at the back of the long, narrow garden set above steep stone steps leading from the back kitchen's yard. He sold the eggs in the Club, and a few chickens at Christmas, with just one kept back for them, and not even that if a last minute drunken request was made over a few too many pints. His own upbringing on a smallholding, curtailed when his father had abandoned it for the wages of a collier in the Edwardian boom years of the Valleys, had stayed with him in the memory and so he had the skills he could bring to bear, from his youth, at harvest time, and in the sheep round-ups of the hill farmers who supplied milk from the churn to the terraced houses below and their animals for the local slaughterhouses. His sour taciturnity suited the need for distance which the farmers liked to keep between themselves on the stony grey outcrops of their tilted fields and the ceaseless clank and thump of the murmurous world of mechanical work which had invaded the valley bottoms like a swarm which would never settle. For his labours he was rewarded not with money but by being given a lamb, or a ewe, or, best of all, a pig whose carcase he would sling over his slight frame to carry down from the mountain and the top-most streets to his riverside terraced house.

He knew how to prepare an animal for butchering. He knew the cuts to make and how to avoid any waste. He had a butcher's cleaver which he kept honed and cleaned for its purpose. He had long-bladed knives for slicing and curved knives for boning. He had short-bladed knives to cut and to gouge and to stick into the animal's parts. The girl saw the pleasure he took in all of this butchery, and with what precise skill he would wield a hand-held blow lamp to remove hair and bristle before cutting off the ears of a pig's eyeless head so that it could be put into boiling water to start to become brawn. He loved that sticky, pungent meat most of all, relishing it for its unmistakable odorous taste, and because the cheapest was, for him, the best.

After the coal industry had been nationalised in 1947, the Union had grown stronger. A delivery of concessionary coal every six months was secured for him. He refused to pay the little extra to have it bagged up, so it came as lump coal. The back lane was too narrow for vehicles to enter and it was dumped from the back of an NCB lorry onto the road, spilling across the pavement, outside his front door. A ton or more of black boulders of coal blocked the pavement and the road until it was taken through the house. First, rough coconut matting had to be laid down in long strips on every surface of its journey from the front door through the house so that as little coal muck and none of the "black pats", glossy backed beetles which might arrive with it from the pit, could dirty or infest the house. All this would be for his inspection later since he had never carried the coal through himself. This, for him, was work for the women. And then the girl.

Piece after piece of the shining, fissured steam coal had to be put into aluminium buckets, two at a time, and carried along the narrow passage, into the middle room, out of the back kitchen, up the stone steps onto the garden path, and then up the garden, past the chicken run, into the shed, to be emptied and stacked, tier by tier, against the back and side walls. It would take her two hours, sometimes more, to do all this after she had come home from school. After his afternoon's drinking sessions, her grandfather would examine her handiwork, her effort, and its result. A grunt would be praise enough. She took care to meet his exacting standards, and to give no excuse for words or blows to rain on her and upset her grandmother.

It was about two years after he had shot and killed "her Nigger" that an unloaded coal delivery would threaten the life of the latest dog he'd acquired. This one was a lurcher, a stiff-haired and brindle-coloured bitch he'd bought from a farmer who often drank with him on Saturday nights. The lurcher was a cross between a whippet and a Bedlington terrier, bred for speed and tenacity in the hunting and catching of rabbits, and vermin. When it was not proving its worth, he kept it tied up in the coal shed by a loose rope knotted to a butcher's wall hook. This dog, for once, had caused no trouble. He called it "Cassie". "After your grandmother" he'd told the girl ; "because she's another beaut, just like you", he'd told his wife. Cassie was no disappointment in herself. What did disappoint him was that, try as he might, he could not interest the girl in the dog. She resolutely refused to pay it any attention.

She carefully managed to be out of his sight whenever she sensed he was going to take Cassie up onto the mountain or down to the riverbank. She shunned the dog if it came near her, imploring her for a look or a touch whenever she fetched coal from the shed for the middle-room's fire or the back kitchen's range. She risked his temper by not feeding the dog when he was not back from the Club on time. And, unlike her indulgence of Tiny and Nigger, both of whom she had sneaked into the house when her grandfather was absent, she obeyed to the strict letter, his injunction not to allow Cassie inside any part of the house. The lurcher always left with him, on any expedition he'd devised, by the back garden gate, and was returned to the shed via the lane.

It was six-thirty when the girl finished her task of taking through the load of coal, stacking it, and cleaning up the fall-out of small coal and dirt. She was bone-tired. Her arms felt stretched by carrying doubled-up buckets. Her leg muscles were strained. Her calves ached after all the hauling. After the final trip she had rolled up and put away the protective matting before brushing down and washing with more buckets of hot, sudsy water, the pavement. She scrubbed the coal dirt from her hands and forearms with a hard bristled hand brush. She used a nail brush to file the coal slurry from underneath her fingernails. She had long since given up trying to pinch out the particles of coal which had burrowed beneath her skin to make unlikely beauty spots of blue on her temple. She poured fresh water from a kettle into the basin and with carbolic soap and a flannel she cleaned her face and swabbed out her nostrils. She blew her nose and rinsed out her mouth before she brushed her hair. She had changed for the task from her school uniform into old clothes and these, in turn, she discarded in the scullery for a later washing. Upstairs, in the mirror of her single wardrobe, she saw how she had grown, how taut her body seemed and how, amongst all the residue of her fatigue, she felt strong, almost a woman.

Downstairs, she filled and boiled a kettle on the range. She put out a wickerwork tray and placed on it a white bone-china cup and saucer, ones decorated with entwined roses of crimson and gold. She poured the hot water onto fresh leaves in the china teapot and let the brew steep. She cut four thin slices of home-baked bread, buttered them and put them together on a plate. The tea was poured through a strainer into the cup and onto the milk, and half a spoon of sugar was added and stirred. She carried the tray up the stairs to the front bedroom where her grandmother lay. Carefully she balanced the tray in the left hand and reached down with her right to turn the dented brass knob to open the panelled and varnished door.

Cassie bounded past her into the room, almost making the girl stumble and drop the tray as the dog ran, in mad circles round and round the bed. The lurcher barked and yelped and jumped up with its hindlegs to put its front paws onto the white counterpane, fully waking up its startled namesake. Cassie's coal blackened paws studded the snowy cover of the bed and smeared it as she jerked up and down and to and fro. Neither the girl nor her grandmother said anything, either to each other, or to the dog.

The girl moved quickly. She put the tray down on the floor beside the bed. She grabbed the dog, bunching up the hair and flesh at the back of its neck to hold it still, to move it, as quickly as she could, out of the house, so that she could return to remove and hide the damage the dog had done. The kitchen door was slightly ajar and, as she pulled the startled lurcher back up the garden she saw that she had left the shed door open after her last trip with the laden buckets. Cassie must have sniffed at an unexpected freedom. The dog had yanked her head out of the rope's noose. The girl tied Cassie tight to the hook this time. She ran back, down the path and the steps and into the kitchen. At the foot of the stairs she heard the voices. He had gone up when he found the doors open. Her grandmother's voice was a low drone of hopeless pleading, his was slurred but loudly insistent.

The girl waited at the bottom of the stairs. She heard a drawer being wrenched open. She heard him curse as he dropped something with a clatter to the floor. She heard a drawer being slammed shut, his stuttering footsteps on the lino-covered landing. Her grandfather appeared at the top of the stairs. He half-fell as he staggered down the carpeted runner, almost slipping on the bottom step where she stood in the passage. He was still dressed for the outdoors. His overcoat was buttoned up over an old suit jacket under which was a flannel shirt and a creamy, fringed muffler around his neck. His black woollen dai cap was set at its customary angle on his head. He grasped the girl's right arm with his left hand, a bony tentacle that pinched hard into her flesh. In his right hand was the Webley pistol. He waved it at his granddaughter who let herself be pulled by the arms as he dragged her through the house to the shed.

He untied the length of rope which had tethered the dog to the hook and he gave it to the girl to hold Cassie whilst he unlocked the back gate of the garden. He pushed her down the lane in the half-dark towards the woods and the river. It had rained heavily the previous day and the river, usually not much more than a wide, sluggish stream, was swollen with the water which had poured into it from the tributary veins which gashed the surrounding hills. The river was unusually full, and it ran by swiftly now in its urgency to empty itself in the distant sea. The rain had stopped overnight but, in the dusk, a prickly chill of washed-out air came down the valley to hang over the rush of the river beside them and drift over the water-filled holes of mud and coal slurry, viscous pools through which they splashed as they went.

The girl felt nothing this time. Not fear nor danger, nor even the cold and the damp amongst the snapping twigs and bare branches of the trees. She and the dog moved faster than him, though they could hear him behind them, warning and threatening them through the gloom. When they reached the mine shaft she held Cassie close to her legs and waited for him. He came on, a little drunk and swaying as he walked towards them. He took Cassie's makeshift lead in his left hand and fumbled in his overcoat pocket for the Webley he'd stuffed in there. It came out the wrong way and it fell to the ground as he dropped it. His daicap slipped off his head as he bent to pick up the gun. He swore and let go of the dog's lead so that he could sink to his knees to retrieve both his gun and his flat cap. His hand clutched at the cap but her foot was firmly on the Webley and she swooped quickly to pick it up herself. Her grandfather looked up, trying to focus on the girl above him, his hand stretching out for her to give him the gun she was holding above her head. She shot him, just once, between his eyes, and he flopped face down in the wet coal waste around the shaft. Cassie sounded a low, whimpering, pathetic noise, and the girl dropped the gun so that she could comfort the dog, her dog now, "her Cassie".

* * * * *

When the dog was safely tied up again in the shed she returned, with night falling, to the disused mine shaft in the woods and to the body she had covered over with fallen leaves. She had taken his wheelbarrow with her, and she used her muscular young arms to lift him and throw his body across it. Once safely back inside the shed, the girl made a hollow space in the middle of the coal pile she had stacked and tiered. She smeared his daicap with his blood and put the Webley in the cap. She shoved his body into the coal pile and closed the hole again. She picked up the cap with the gun inside and walked again through the woods to the river, to a steep bank a mile or so downstream of the shaft. She threw them, close but separate, down the steep and slippery embankment, where he'd shot himself, drunk but grieving over his wife's incurable cancer, fell into the river and been swept away. He was never to be found. He had stayed out overnight before, carousing with his friends, so she had had no reason to be alarmed, or to have woken her ill grandmother. It was why she could wait until the next day, late afternoon, to tell a neighbour her grandfather was still not home. They would tell the police. She had felt elated, not tired at all, as she walked home again to the shed where she knew she needed to finish matters so that her own story could begin. So she pulled his shrunken body from its black hole and she took off his clothes.

On the butcher's block he kept against a side wall, she spread out his limbs. She balanced the cleaver for its weight and then she brought it down as cleanly and as forcefully as she could. The edge he had honed did the rest and whatever, arms and legs and hands and feet, which she did not sever with a single blow she hatcheted and chopped and sawed and sliced so that he came to bits, piece by piece, as chest and breastbone and knobbly knees and ganglions and sinews. She gouged out his eyes with a curved blade and some skewers and fed them to the dog along with his internal organs. Cassie gobbled and slurped. Her mistress placed the bits and pieces into two hessian sacks and weighted them down with the heaviest lumps of coal she could handle. She waited until it was pitch black outside to take her parcels to a deep quarry pool, green and glacially cold, where he had often drowned kittens and puppies, for himself and for others, in earlier years. She had put the clothes she had cut away into the coal-burning kitchen range's furnace where they would burn to a cinder, and to the ash she would rake away in the morning. Into the early hours she scrubbed and washed and washed and scrubbed as she had been so well taught to do. The head, which she had cut off at the neck with an executioner's practised chop, she had decided to keep. It was put back into the hold she had made amongst the coal. The rain was falling heavily again.

She was finally exhausted by all her labour. She slept soundly, her dog nestled alongside her at the foot of her bed. When they woke she took the lurcher back to the shed, and left her loose. Her grandmother was still asleep in the early dawn. The girl decided she would have a treat later, as a surprise. She would make her some brawn, the meat her grandmother had loved as much as her husband. Perhaps it was a generation thing. In the larder was a pig's head he'd prepared the previous day. The girl knew whenever she had been given the brawn made from the eyeless and earless and hairless head that the texture and savour of it would never be for her but, for those older others, it was a memory food, a re-call as much as a sustenance. It was how, it seemed, in these simple recurrent moments of smell and touch and sensation that they measured the repetitive downward tick of their lives.

In the kitchen the girl found the large aluminium stock pot her grandmother had habitually used and filled it with cold water. When it had bubbled long enough she added several handfuls of cooking salt and took the pot off the heat to cool down. She made toast and tea for breakfast and took her grandmother's upstairs. His absence caused no comment, only a shrug of the sick woman's frail shoulders. She presumed the dog had been punished and her husband to be drunk. No surprises there. The girl went back to the kitchen. She dropped the pig's head she took from the larder into the stock pot and she took the discarded ears for Cassie to eat. She heard her dog whimper, with delight now, whenever she approached.

In the shed she reached into the hole for her grandfather's head. She set its mangled shape squarely on the block. His thin wispy hair was matted in places with his dried blood and elsewhere was still slicked down with the vaseline he had spread from the palms of his hands to his scalp so that he could part it neatly on one side. He was, as ever, closely and cleanly shaven by his cut-throat razor, so she could ignore that aspect. She took down his blow lamp from the shelf. She pumped the hand piston to make the paraffin flow. She used a Swan's Vesta match to light it and she adjusted the flame, in the way she had seen him do, so that it would burn the hair of his head off without singeing it. She worked swiftly on his hair, as he had done with the pig's bristle. The lurcher had eaten the old man's wrinkled ears she had sliced off the night before. The tang of paraffin was heavy in the shed, and she felt warm.

In the kitchen she washed his head – the false teeth had burned in the furnace with his clothes – under a fast-running tap before it was plunged into the brine alongside that of the pig's he had already made ready. She put a plate over the pot and replaced it on its shelf in the cold larder. She calculated the twenty four hours she would need to wait for it to be ready for the next stage. The police would be searching for him by then: on the mountain, at the riverbank, in the river. Everywhere. But not in the pot. She kissed her grandmother goodbye and went to school. When she came home she waited until after six to wonder about his whereabouts with her grandmother and the next door neighbour.

The following day, all agreed, she did not need to go to school. She could stay at home to make cups of tea for whoever called and to see to her grandmother's needs. In any case, she was up early to walk Cassie. She had drained the heads well before dawn. She quartered them now with his sharpest butcher's knife and covered them again with cold water and yet more salt. She added to the water some roughly chopped carrots and four halved onions from his allotment, and whole peppercorns and a few cloves and lots of fresh thyme from his garden. She boiled the pot until it simmered. Periodically, she skimmed off flecks of beige and brown scum from its surface. It had to bubble away quietly for four hours, her grandmother's exact recipe time, being topped up with water whenever the meat was not covered.

Callers to the house, upstairs with her grandmother or sat in the best front room with cups of tea and digestive biscuits, remarked on the evoking smell from the kitchen and how she was such a good girl to be so busy making brawn for her grandmother, whose favourite it also was. A piece or two would be sure to do her some good at this worrying time.

When there were no more visitors and no further police enquiries being made at the house she took out the broad wooden board on which pastry was rolled, and on it she put the drained heads from which the meat was now falling. She pulled it away further by hand. With a small pointed knife she cut roundels of meat from the cheek bones and when all the meat was off the heads she mixed it all up and chopped it finely, all together, with a small mountain of fresh parsley he had bought for his own purpose, now to be hers. The girl filled a big, white pudding bowl right to its rim and with her hands again, pressed the meats firmly down into the bowl. Earlier she had strained the cooled cooking liquor which she slowly poured over the shredded meat mixture. When it was swamped by the slick liquid she rammed a small plate within the rim of the bowl so that the liquor was displaced around the edges of the plate. She weighted the plate down even further with the round iron weights of the old balance weighing machine they still used. She knew it would need a further twelve hours to settle and be finished in the dark larder. At the back, on the stone, where it was coldest. The bones and all the rest sizzled in the fire.

Her grandfather's friend, the one who had found the gun for him, came to see them a couple of days later after he'd been to the Legion where, he said, her grandfather's memory would be forever sacred. He said that the police had found the Webley and his bloodied cap. The rain had washed the bank further away and they were at the river's edge. That, he was sorry to say, it really did look like he'd killed himself, worried sick, no doubt, about his dear wife, poor Cassie. He had had a load of drink that day, too, sad to say, but there you are, and all that, and didn't we all sometime. Anyway, also, at the Club they'd decided there'd be a Collection. In due course. Oh, and one more thing, best not to mention, say anything about, the gun, where it might have come from, and all that, origins, see? And he winked, and looked at her, and gave her a dusty pink ten bob note. The first money she'd earned.

The girl gave him a cup of tea. He had asked for milk and two sugars. She had sat him in the kitchen in her grandfather's old chair. She told him her grandmother was asleep, again, upstairs. Not long now, the Doctor had said. He nodded twice and stirred the sugar in his tea. On the table she had inverted the deep, white pudding basin onto a plate, and removed the bowl. On the plate was the mound of pink and brown gelatinous brawn. It was marbled through by the parsley like the floating moss green strands adrift after the rains in the slow-moving river. He asked her if she'd made that, looked lovely it did, bet it tasted good, too. The girl smiled. She said her grandmother had managed a mouthful or two but that she didn't like brawn herself, and there was far too much for the two of them, so would he like to try some? The girl cut two pieces of bread from a white loaf, and buttered them. She carved a generous slice of the home-made brawn and put it, with the bread, onto a plate of the best china.

Her grandfather's drinking companion, the gun-supplier, took the fork she gave him and put it into the meat. He raised the portion to his mouth. He ate, and swallowed. He ate some more. He opened his bleary eyes wider. That, he told her, was the tastiest bit of brawn he'd eaten since before the war. It was the bloody real thing, that was, and she must give him the recipe so that his old woman could make some. Perfect it was. He'd have some more, if he may. He might. The girl smiled, grateful for the praise, and cut him off a further slice. She slid it onto his place and, underneath the table, she fed a more delicate piece of the brawn to Cassie, "her Cassie", who licked the girl's capable hands and rubbed herself against the girl's strong and steady legs.

Socratic Dialogue

"So tell me the backstory," he said.

"There is no backstory," I said.

"Whaddya mean there's no backstory, you schmuck. There's always a backstory," he said.

"Not this time. Not so far as I know," I said.

"So far as you know? So far as you know? That's a fuckin' comfort, then," he said.

"Look," I said. "The point is that where I'm concerned this is the beginning. And the end, too. Sorry. End of story."

"You think it's an end for you? It may be an end for me, all right, you creep," he said. "For you, it's another story. A backstory in the making. A personal one to you," he said. "D'you think you can file this away under Contract Fulfilled, Fees Paid, or something? D'you think you won't store this in the shallow recess of your peanut sized brain pan? Where it will, I assure you, fester my dear friend. Guaranteed. You hear? You have my personal guarantee on that."

I said nothing. He sighed as if I was a lousy student.

"D'you understand, nothing?" he said.

I looked at him closely for the first time. I really looked at him as he sat, naked and awkwardly, on the grey silk counterpane of his king size bed in the exclusive five star hotel in its downtown waterfront location. You don't want to know what he looked like, really looked like I mean. What would be the point? For you, I mean. Like I said, like I told him, there was no backstory.

It would have been better if he hadn't woken up. I had let myself in, just before dawn, with my very desirable universal pass key. He had drawn the heavy curtains in the room but I could make out his shape in the bed. I had, you know, half expected there to be a woman in bed with him. That would have meant two-for-the-price-of-one. But there was no woman. So, good I thought, he's alone. He just woke up. Maybe he was a light-sleeper.Maybe old habits die hard. I don't know.I do know I'd made no noise.He put on the bedside lamp , and sat up and saw me standing over him with the Beretta sticking out from my left hand, longer with the attached silencer screwed on.I waved it at him to make sure he stayed still. He didn't seem scared. He didn't panic. That was my problem, right there. He didn't seem anything. As if it was all the most natural thing in the world. I guess it was for me, too. Only reverse image in the mirror, right? He swung his legs out of the bed and sat there, staring. I shouldn't have hesitated, I know, but he looked really interested in me, really inquisitive. That was a new thing for me. A problem, maybe.

"D'you know who I am?" he said.

That was the first thing he said, and I said, "No." Maybe I shouldn't have answered him in the first place. Then he did all that stuff about the backstory, and I fell for it because I really didn't have any backstory for this, and maybe, I can see now, I wanted one. Maybe everybody wants one, you know. He'd look at me, and it was almost with pity. It was as if I didn't have a real enough life without a backstory. He obviously had one. He sighed again.

"OK, I'll tell you the backstory, then," he said.

"Fill you in. On what you don't seem to know."

"Don't bother," I said, and I transferred the gun to my right hand. The palm of my left hand began to leave a fine, damp sweat on the black dimpled stock of the gun. It was hot in the room. He hadn't adjusted the air conditioning overnight. He seemed cool enough himself.

"I wonder," he said. "You're not just some punk, are you? Some clown breaking in for some smash-and-grab robbery, helped by the maid with a key, after cash – you could have that from me, you know – are you?"

I said nothing again.

He said, "No. Pity. I didn't think so."

"On the other hand," he said, "for you to be so ignorant, about me, means, to me, that you're not really worthy of walking away from this with the only thing really worth having. And that is my very particular backstory. Of which, bird brain, you are now a part, like it or not, know it or not. Now I can live, or die, with all that because, precisely because, I do know. I know it all now. And that includes you. You are just a piece of late debris floating in on the far spectrum of my existence."

"Not stretching your vocabulary too much, am I?" he said.

He opened up his hands to show me his palms. There was no sweat.

"Let's look at it this way," he said. "I could be an accountant, a crooked one naturally, or a politician, bribed and corrupt naturally, or a husband, cheating and caught out of course, or, think of this, you schmuck, an innocent victim of the malign intent of others, for whom you are a handy patsy?"

"Don't call me a schmuck again," I said.

This time he laughed. Out loud. I waved the Beretta at him again. Maybe I should have pointed it straight at him. But I didn't.

"That's better, pal, isn't it?" he said. "Get a little heated to get a little light. And my guess is you have more than a glimmer of that, already."

"See," he said, "because you say you don't know a thing doesn't mean you can't know a thing even when, strictly speaking, you really don't know. Only, in your case, I'm saying, surmising if you will, that if you think you don't know you think you don't need to care. But then because you may indeed not know what you don't want to know you didn't want me to wake up, did you? Because then, O buddy mine, and believe me I can see it's a problem for you, and I appreciate that, then you, you in particular, really do care, don't you?"

He was beginning to look smug. He was beginning to annoy me. He was not going to stop. I could see that. He'd have to be stopped. Some time soon. He was still asking questions.

"Now why, I wonder, is this? Is it because, underneath it all, you're just a schlemiel? Nah, I didn't think so. And it's not because of my cute face, my enticing voice, my baby blues. And, anyway, you haven't heard me beg or plead with you, have you, paisan?"

He swallowed. As if there was some neat resolution to this. Other than the one he thought was otherwise coming.

"I'll tell you why," he said, "and you won't like it, but here it is, bozo, it's because, for you, from here on in, not knowing, and therefore being able to do whatever it is you get to do, is no longer enough. It doesn't matter about me anymore. This is about us now. You're a part of me. That's the backstory which matters, friend. You're me, too, and you won't like that whatever happens. You won't like it, and you can't stop it. It's guaranteed. You have my personal warranty on that."

With that he shifted his buttocks on the bed. He kept his hands on his knees and his eyes on my face. He never looked at the gun. Not once. He was about six feet away from where I was standing. He wasn't sweating. He seemed in no hurry about anything. I moved the gun back into my preferred hand. Just an instant. I saw his eyes flicker. He saw that I saw that.

"I'm not fucking with you, compadre. That's just the way it is. For all of us."

I tightened my finger on the trigger. Time to move on. No backstory, no matter what he thinks. Not for me. And certainly not,anymore, for him. This edition of the story was coming to an end. I think he saw that too. When he spoke now it was in a tone drained of bravado.

"I'm coming at this the wrong way, I can see that now," he said. "Maybe we should forget my backstory. You're right about that. What is it to you? What's done is done and maybe I have no fast-forward button left to push."

He pointed the index finger of his right hand at me. I didn't like that. His finger was poised in the air.

"But, what I'm saying is," he said, "is that you do. Have a future, I mean. What's it to be? To know that, you have to know your own backstory. "The unexamined life is not worth having." Do you know who said that first? Socrates. Or rather, Socrates was the mouthpiece for the guy who thought about it. Plato. Greeks. Ancient Greeks. I got to read a lot, hanging around, waiting, in my profession. Excuse me, our profession.

"For a man who reads a lot, you talk too much," I told him.

That amused him. Perhaps he thought I was hooked.

"So you tell me about your backstory," he said. "I bet I could guess most of it even. Take those pretty blue scars on your face. Coal miners get those. But you've never been underground, have you? Not that kind of underground anyway. But you've lived near enough to the life one way or other, haven't you? It's a backstory, see. And your accent, not of this city I can tell, even with my tin American ear, but local enough I'd guess, so they knew I'd be coming and they didn't have time for anyone really from out-of-town. It's a story in reverse, ain't it?"

It was my turn to swallow now. Too loud. Too obvious.

"And do you know how and why I can do this, make a guess that connects?" he said. "Because, in essentials, it'll be the same backstory as mine. Leave or take a few details of no consequence about doting mothers and abusive fathers or crazy bitches or the drone of dreams in some rural backwater or worked-out coalfield or maybe the Army, or maybe just haywire genes. It's what happens after all that, isn't it, which matters. The whys and the wherefores. You know where I'm coming from now, don't you?" he said.

"This is pointless," I said. "You're just prolonging the time left."

For the first time he looked interested in me.

"Prolong, eh?" he said. "Not pass the time or waste the time, just prolong?"

"Well, kiddo," he said. "I'm long past the prolongation stage. If this is it, this here and now, so be it. I can cash in anytime. I've assembled enough chips to leave with a balance in credit."

He stopped, quite abruptly, as if the disbelief on my face had really registered with him.

"Oh, God," he said. "You really don't get it, do you?"

He shifted uneasily on the bed. His old wrinkled balls seemed swollen, with his penis curled back into the cleft of their sack like a pink slug. He scratched at it, and shuffled a bit more towards me. He took a deep breath as if I was going to be more difficult to reach, in every way, than he'd first thought. He was right about that. I knew that for nothing.

"Let us assume," he said, "that our positions were reversed. Retro. Verso. Then, you might ask, would I need to know your backstory? Or want to? And you'd be right, except for idle curiosity, which I've never had. I would not. Are we converging on this?"

"No," I said.

He said, "Mmm. OK. Well, let's put it another way. The older you are, like me, the more interested, in a deeper sense than being curious, you are about what is past. Because what is past will certainly be more than what is yet to come. Even, in this sense, your past, for me. That past, shall we say, is what is sustaining this particular moment in present time. It certainly, how did you put it? prolongs it. So, yes, I'd say, if positions were reversed you would like to know my backstory and, since they are not, as yet, I'd be happy to learn more about yours than anything, I might guess."

"Want to try?" he said. "Show me yours and I'll tell you mine, and all that malarkey."

"No," I said.

I think he was enjoying himself. That he could see that the kind of prolonging which he wanted was happening after all.

"Can't blame me for trying, can you?" he said.

I shrugged. Trying was not the same as succeeding was what I thought.

"Besides", he said, and very smartly this time, "you haven't ended our conversation yet, have you? Why not?"

That was a dangerous question to ask. The truth was I didn't know why not. Perhaps it was because I hadn't had any kind of conversation in quite a while. I hesitated, and then I said:

"You're not what I expected."

"I'm not what you expected," he said, "and what exactly, by the way, were your expectations?"

"That it'd be over by now. All over, I mean," I said.

"Dead is what you actually mean," he said. "That I'd be dead, never having woken up."

He got the hole in one with that. The waking up part, I mean. That had changed the game. Usually, they were too distant or it was too quick to bother me. His waking had spooked me. He kept his stare too long for my liking. The time of his particular time, oh boy, that was ticking fast.

"Wait," he said. "I'm going to tell you something important."

"Bear with me", he said. "I'm just trying to think of how best to tell you, to explain it to you. So, I'm going to try an analogy."

I knew what that was. I didn't know why I wanted to hear it.

"You know what an analogy is, don't you?" he said. "Well this one is about another kind of encounter. A battle. One without obvious winners and losers at the start. Though, for sure, there will be a pre-destined winner and a doomed loser by its end. And the reason for that is not just what actually happens in the encounter, in the battle, but what makes it happen at all, what frames its outcome. Heroism. Decision. Sacrifice. Mistakes. Yeah, all that, of course, but can it alter things without, you know what I'm going to say, a backstory?"

He made a fingertip cathedral arch, and examined it. He unfolded it and put his hands, palms down, on his thighs.

"I'm a student," he said, "or, you might say, an old buff, an obsessive, about the Battle of Gettysburg, July first to July third, 1863. Pennsylvania. The bloody, bloody American Civil War. That battle, did you know, was the last time that sovereign United States territory was invaded. By the Army of Northern Virginia, the name used, with all its local pride and limitations, for the whole of the invading force which was, indeed, the Grand Army of all of the states who had seceded to form the rebel Confederacy in 1861. There were about eighty thousand fighting men, with around another twenty to thirty thousand non-combatants, mostly blacks, negro slaves, working as cooks and porters and general factotums. The Army, that proud instrument of Alabama as well as Virginia, of Texas as well as Georgia, of the Carolinas and Mississippi, and all of that honourable, self-deluding culture that was the South, was led by the incarnation of that South: the fifty six year old Robert E. Lee, Christian gentleman of Virginia, outwardly reserved, inwardly cavalier, and the era's most dazzling, professional commander."

I looked at him again. At the fuzzy muss of his white hair and the grey stubble of his early morning beard and the watery pale blue eyes that were seeing something outside the room. I thought, old man, you're at least fifty six and you've never been anything like Robert E. Lee. He didn't seem bothered either way. It was his story, and he was going to tell it. If I let him.

"Kid", he said, "Lee felt the whole thing falling into his hands. With one effort, of power and genius, he could turn the war. Threaten Washington, just up the road, and make Lincoln sue for peace. The Armies were converging. Just as he wanted. Soon at that insignificant cross-roads town, a burg really, of Gettysburg, he would be opposed by the Army of the Potomac, another geographically restricted name for the major armed force of the Union's battered administration. It would march towards Lee's unexpected concentration, and do so under the command of its new, very new, just a few days in fact, leader. The decidedly uncharismatic, untested, extremely cautious, General George Gordon Meade, forty three years old, and like Lee a pre-war Democrat, albeit of the Union kind, but, for sure, no Republican, a reluctant warrior, like so many of the top brass in his Army."

He looked straight at me again. Back with me. He clasped his hands together, and wrung them gently.

"Don't worry. I can see you don't want to waste time. And I have no intention, even in the interest of my prolonged good health, to turn into the Scheherazade of Gettysburg as you beg for more and more detail, eked out over a thousand nights. I'll pare it down. To the bone, OK, Reb?"

I'd decided there was no rush. It was decided. I'd not retreat.

"Right", he said. "What came together were two mighty forces, but one by choice was there and the other was drawn to it as if by a magnet. Lee had gathered up all the strength, in arms and men, that he could muster, in order to take the war to the Yankees, to the Union states across the border, and in their own territory. Only a resounding victory, he had argued, would confound the enemy who, otherwise, would eventually out-muscle and out-wait the poorer South. If he could win, no, he must win, Lee felt northern public opinion would become so restless that the unpopular Lincoln would be forced to make a peace overture. One that would lead to the agreed independence of the Confederate States of America. What a world-changing moment that would have been, huh?"

Since I said nothing, he looked to engage me another way. To bring us together, in spirit, or practice at least.

"You must read, don't you? I mean in our profession there's a lot of waiting about, isn't there? Or maybe, I forget about the young sometimes, you just play some mindless game or other. Pity. Because, Einstein, if you bothered to read you might have read that inspirational sot and Nobel Prize Winner, William Faulkner whose great grandfather, William T. Falkner of Mississippi, fought in that battle, when Lee on the final day sent General Pickett's massed infantry across the fields and up to the ridge where Union guns halted their wave after wave and sent them crashing back in disarray to defeat. But when they set out, thousands upon thousands of them in their homespun butternut grey, shouldering their rifles, keeping in step as their comrades randomly fell by their side, when they started out in the heat of that July afternoon, everything, I mean everything, was still at stake, still to play for. That's why the great novelist, the great grandson would say, speaking for all his lost kind, that for every Southern boy it was still not yet two o'clock on that July afternoon in 1863 and no, he means, nothing had been decided, and yes, he means everything had been so decided. All of subsequent life, even as it was weighed in the balance."

"You see," he said, "the gallant Pickett did charge because the driven Lee wanted it so, but Lee's second-in-command, General James Augustus Longstreet, who did not want it so, delayed and delayed in releasing Pickett, until some thought and think, he'd left it all too late. Longstreet had thought they were to fight a tactically defensive, attritional battle with the Federal forces, not an aggressive, full-frontal attack, a gamble for glory or disaster. Lee gambled, and Lee lost."

"But here's the rub," he said. "He might never have gambled if, on the first day, as the rival armies found themselves unexpectedly meeting up, a Union Major-General, John Reynolds, dead on the battlefield at forty three, had not intervened to hold up Lee's advance brigades, despite the few mounted troopers at his disposal before Meade's sluggish main body of infantry and artillery, could turn up."

He wiped his lips with his left hand, and used his right to wag that index finger at me. Too many people had done that to me, all my life. Did he know that, too?

"Reynolds was just," he said, "with an advance cavalry detachment as a probe, scouting ahead, when he stumbled across the forward troops of the entire Army of Northern Virginia on the first of July. The logic would have been retreat. But Reynolds saw that if he did not hold his ground for a few hours in the town then any retreat after that to the desirable hills and ridges around the town to the south and east would be over-run, and those sweet heights would be in Lee's hands. The heights, Cemetery Hill and Seminary Ridge, where Pickett's charge would die would instead serve Lee to rout Meade's oncoming army.

"Now, follow me closely, here. Listen up."

People had regretted asking me to do that, before now. Should I tell him that? Or did he also know that, too?

"You see," he said, "Reynolds was actually under orders to retreat if he came across the enemy. Meade did not wish to advance. He wanted to wait, elsewhere, seventeen miles away from Gettysburg. It was Reynolds who forced Meade's hand by pulling Lee into a fire fight before Lee was fully ready to spring his trap. Reynolds called up more infantry and engaged the enemy. Meade then had to march to the sound of the guns, and the destiny he feared.

"Enough," he said. "Enough. That's all just events and I promised you a backstory. The backstory is that of John Reynolds. Why did he bring it on? In defiance of Meade? Why? Because he was a native of south-central Pennsylvania. This was his soil that was being invaded. The time had come. It was a mirror image of Lee, who fought for Virginia more than he did the South, and who wanted, if he could manage it, no more suffering on Virginian soil. Bring it on, indeed. And when it was done and Lee, broken and guilt-racked, pulled back across the mountain gaps into the Shenandoah Valley, Meade, consensual and nervous, did not follow. His backstory. All backstories are inescapable, you just have to know how to read them."

Like you're assuming you can read mine, I thought.

"All endings have their origins," I said.

"But," I said. "Not all beginnings have to be found in those endings."

He straightened his back. He cocked his head to the side.

"That," he said, "is where you and me may be at this very moment."

"But what is this moment, exactly?" he said.

It wasn't a question.

"It's now, of course," he said, "but it's also what can be avoided, or induced. You have no choice, other than to leave or stay. It will be how you will meet this moment. My point has been, and I know you see it, that if you choose to stay you take on the backstory that begins again, the one you cannot avoid after you act, the one that will sweep you on. Believe me, I know. I've been there. I've even seen this moment coming. For me, I mean. Not exactly like this, but close enough to recognise it. The luck is you woke me so that, chico, I can show you what it means. I think you've seen it coming too. What will it be, an end or a beginning?"

I moved towards him. He didn't seem concerned. I extended my left hand, the one still holding the Beretta, so that the gun barrel centred on the middle of his forehead. If he flinched, I didn't see it. I lowered the gun. I transferred it to my right and held it so that the stock was turned towards him. I waited. He made no move. He seemed to have considered what would have been, truly, an unfeasible choice. He was right. I would have finished it. So, I nodded and I walked away from him with my back turned. I waited, an instant, one last time. I said "OK then", and I put the gun down on an occasional table set in the corner of the room. It lay there, posed, amongst a scatter of glossy magazines. I turned to face him. He was puzzled for the first time. Me, I was certain for the last time.

"You forgot something, old man," I said.

He raised an eyebrow. Irritated.

"Enlighten me, punk," he said.

"That General Longstreet," I said.

"Yes?" he said, as if I was really an eager pupil.

"He could have made Gettysburg different, couldn't he?" I said. "I mean if he'd persuaded Lee not to attack against the guns in those positions. If he'd found alternative, defensive positions. If he'd made Meade fight only when Lee was ready, and where Longstreet wanted. If they'd left Gettysburg behind them and outflanked Meade, and if they'd kept their invasion going …"

"If, if, if", he said, and "maybe".

"Then", I said, "there would have been no backstory to trap them. No backstory to haunt and hurt and define and confuse and destroy."

"There's always a backstory, sunshine," he said. "You haven't been listening, have you?"

"Yeah, I have," I said.

"And," I said, "my humble conclusion, not being so book-read as you, is that we don't, ever, have to pick up on the only backstory there is, or seems to be. We can make our own up. Some of the time anyway. And this time will be mine, old man."

"Don't patronise me, you fuck", he said.

"I'm leaving", I said. "But the gun stays. I'm leaving. But you aren't going anywhere, are you? Your backstory has to have the ending you're going to give it, doesn't it? Or something like. But thanks, Teacher, you've made mine different now. And complete, too."

I backed away from him, more cautiously this time, towards the door. I'd made sure I was still nearer to the gun when I touched the door handle than he was to the side table where the gun still waited.

"If not you today, who tomorrow?" he said.

"If not me tomorrow, why not you today?" I said.

I opened the door and stepped into the corridor. I locked the door, as if it mattered. I walked down the thickly carpeted corridor to the lift at its end. I pressed the Down button on the wall. I waited. I heard the elevator arrive and its doors make a clunky, opening sound. I stepped in. Down the corridor, back from where I'd come I heard a single, muffled shot. I said "Croeso, butt" out loud, and then I pressed the Ground Floor button to take me down to the foyer. I walked across the bluey slate floor, my high heels clicking in rhythm with my sway. I went out into the night,just another night or, just maybe, one that was becoming a different kind of dawn.I didn't bet on it.

Not Anna

The class met at eleven every Thursday morning. She had to take two buses to get there, one leaving the valley at nine and the other from the city centre at 10.15, then a five minutes walk to be on time. She was always on time. She had never missed a class. They met in one of the older buildings still left on the campus. It was a single storey, pseudo-Gothic affair, a kind of extended gallery in locally quarried and block-hewn stone which had been tacked onto the Romantic pile, turrets and towers, which the Copper King had commissioned for his parkland in the 1850s. The pile was now a warren of pokey offices and draughty reception rooms, and the gallery had been sub-divided into class rooms for seminars. Each room was separated, along the length of a parquet-floor corridor, by lath-and-plaster walls with half-glass doors set at intervals into the corridor wall. The furnishings inside each room – liberal arts teaching only – were minimal. A scatter of wooden chairs with desk-arms, a table and chair at the front and behind them a whiteboard on an otherwise bare wall. External light came from two long, original and mullioned windows looking out onto a terrace set slightly above the rolling slopes of the campus, whilst a fitful internal illumination came from a fly-specked fluorescent tube fixed to the ceiling.

Christine was the first to arrive. She clicked the switch to put the flickering overhead light on against the outside wintry gloom. Christine liked being early. She liked sitting there alone, her chosen chair positioned to be slightly to one side, waiting for the others. There were usually around eight of them, depending on illness or family commitments or holidays, and, of course, there was the Tutor, Derek Holdsworth B.A (Cantab), D.Phil (Oxon). Christine had had to look up the meaning of the letters put after his name in the university's brochure for Lifelong Learning. Now she knew them, and their meaning, as if by heart and she said them to herself, quietly and warmly, by respectful rote. Cantab and Oxon. Oxford and Cambridge. From the photographs she had seen in the coffee-table books she'd borrowed from the library, she felt she could almost touch, in her mind, that blend of the antique and the aesthetic which the images of colleges and quads and rivers and punts and gowns and spires laid before her in their page flattened dimension. Perhaps a coach trip would be possible in the summer if she could find someone to stay with her mother for a couple of days. Or rather if she could persuade her mother to agree to it. Christine looked out of the windows of the classroom at the jumble of uniform glass and steel boxes and residential tower blocks strewn across the campus. It had begun to snow. Christine liked the waiting. She savoured the anticipation of what was to come.

Ten people had originally registered for the weekly two hour long class on 'The Realist Novel: Love and Society in the Nineteenth Century'. Two of them, both men as it happened, had dropped out after the second of the twenty sessions scheduled over two terms. The eight who remained were all women, mostly in their late sixties or, like Christine, just into that decade of life with only Diana Lewry still in her, rather striking they all agreed, mid-forties. Oddly enough, Christine considered, she was more at ease with Diana than the others who were all wives or widows of former faculty staff and seemed to her proprietorial, almost as a collective, about the existence of such a class in the first place. Something perhaps to pass the time they had no choice now but to pass. Together. Christine knew that this was no choice for her, but a chance like no other she had ever had. She sensed how her serious intent was not, by them, so well regarded. Not so by Diana Lewry though who stood out for other reasons. Relative youth and undeniable good looks for a start. Coal-black hair and hazel-flecked eyes, and a trimness of figure her short skirts and tightly-hugging jumpers were not devised to disguise, was a part of it, but also because, like Christine, she had, from the start, engaged with the literature. The faculty women were rapt enough in their attention but quiescent in response. Christine had thought, at first, that she would be too shy, too inexperienced, too intimidated, to rise to the tutor's bait of question-and-answer, yet the tug of her interest was, she found, irresistibly strong and especially when Diana led the way with common sense replies to Derek Holdsworth's compound of acerbic wit and intellectual commentary. Over the first term the pattern became set and then accepted. Diana and Derek, with Diana invariably ready to concede the point, would bat this or that thought or consideration back and fro until, to a general sense of amused relief, Christine, flustered but persistent, would make it an unlikely threesome. The others, put out to winter grass in this extra mural tradition, just as they would putt or bowl on other grass courses when summer released them, would murmur or titter, always appreciatively, depending on who was currently speaking. The relationship between them and their tutor was well-established for they had attended his classes before, and over coffee in the break after the first hour, he would ask, pleasantly enough, how his Grass Widows were doing, and of the health of any of the husbands who had lived on into retirement after the rigours of academic life. That was not as it was, they all agreed. Whereas, Diana Lewry as the wife of a G.P recently moved into the area and Christine Verity as a recently retired local government officer were indeed different, welcomed but on the edge of the group and its own particular purpose.

When the class first met, Derek Holdsworth had told them of the novels he had chosen for study and the inexpensive paperback editions he wished them to buy. They were to read the editor's explanatory Notes but, for the present, to ignore the fuller Introductions or Forewords. "Too prescriptive," he'd laughed and, smiling at Diana, added "Even for a Doctor's wife, Mrs Lewry." There were, nonetheless, other hand-outs from him, of contemporary quotations and criticism, along with a page-long bibliography of texts meant to establish, he said knowingly as if he was speaking in inverted commas, the "all important context". The essence of the novels, he stressed, would be for them to discover for themselves. The text was itself the adventure, the journey, on which they were, and here a wink to show his awareness of the cliché he would only use as such, "now embarked". He was sure, he said, that the insights they would bring to the works by being themselves women in an unresolved contemporary setting would reveal the feminist struggles and patriarchal stifling of the past as laid out in "these great novels". Perhaps the two male attendees felt themselves superfluous after this, and left the group shortly after it had begun to explore the fictional world of four famous women.

They had started with *Madame Bovary* and followed it before Christmas, with *Middlemarch*. Christine had read neither book before, and had not even heard of the latter whose sheer size daunted her as she weighed it in her hands. She had been excited by the Flaubert, initially disturbed by so much that remained startlingly illicit in its sexually charged undercurrent, but the Eliot confounded her by its intellectual challenge set alongside its drab accounting, or was it more its accounting for the drab. Under Dr Holdsworth's guidance they had been taken down paths of style and intent, through by-ways of characterisation and contemporary context until, piece by piece, Christine saw, for the first time, things as a whole and fragments as mosaics to place how and where she could. The more she understood the more, to her surprise, was she personally moved. The mystery of understanding at all was not taken away by the education, as she had half-wanted, it was given a depth and force that made its power all the more mysterious, almost unattainable or perhaps undesirable as a finished object. Her emotions, confronted by reading and discussing and re-reading, switch- backed from sympathy to empathy, from dislike to despair, as Charles and Emma and Dorothea and Casaubon and Lydgate and Rosamund , performed and re-played their fixed, or was it fated,marital destinies. In their presence Christine had never felt more sensitive to both the pulses and the deadened nerves of her own past and continuing life.

Now, waiting and alone, in late January at the beginning of the second term, with snow falling yet more heavily, each fresh fall making the icy slush beneath more treacherous, she tapped the laminated cover of the next masterpiece with the bitten nail of her right-hand index finger. She drummed a beat on the lovely face of Anna Karenina, or rather on the portrait of the society beauty chosen by the publisher to represent Anna, and she looked forward, with the Russian novel already finished, to Zola's *Nana*, yet to come. But that could wait. The Tolstoy, which had been opened on New Year's Day and consumed within three weeks, had, and she did not quite know how as yet, worried her. She was rarely disturbed by anything anymore. Yet now she was, and her anticipation of how that might be explained was acute. She had not been able to counterpoint her feelings with the kind of discussion which had ordered such matters so distinctly for her before the Christmas break. Adrift from the class and the fierce clarity of Derek Holdsworth's knowledge, she had had only herself to consult. She could not, of course, discuss it with her mother who, in any case, resented any moment she saw Christine sitting down to read, not being useful as she'd always put it. So she read of Anna and of Karenin, and of Vronsky, in between preparing meals for the two of them, and cleaning and shopping. She read in bursts when her mother, satisfied and silent at last, sat transfixed by a soap or reality show on television. She read mostly in bed, holding the bulky paperback as steady as she could above her counterpane.

She saw herself as someone in training, like a sportsperson almost, for the new season when the Coach, the tutor, Dr Holdsworth, Derek of Cantab and Oxon, would take the whole team on a strategic tour of the circumstances around the whole book before canvassing individual opinion and queries. The ground laid out in this way he would then, she knew, tease out, week by week, their understanding of his own sophisticated, and complete, rendition of the great work he would, if they cared to,allow them to possess for themselves. Though she had been flummoxed at first by this method of teaching – his pedagogical penance , he'd called it with his customary wink to the class – Christine had come to feel as privileged as a novitiate being prepared to enter an exclusive Order. Nothing was made easy after the easy, assured eloquence of his opening foray into life and times and culture. Once that clutter, his irony again they intuited , was cleared away he would sit before them, his expressive and tapered fingers drumming gently on the plain deal table at which he sat, until he drove them, forced them, or was it that he seduced them, into breaking the silence. The others were more than happy to allow him to raise an eyebrow and glance in Diana Lewry's direction. She would make the dialogue less that of a supplicant before a master, more like a playful bout of badinage with the result never in doubt. Christine, however hard she tried to rein in her eagerness, could not help but sound a querulous tone in her genuine impatience for an answer. This time, with this book, her anxiety was becoming more acute, her expectation more strained. She could scarcely wait. She had a question to ask about Anna.

Christine had not thought, when she signed up for the literature course at the University's Lifelong Learning Centre upon her retirement from the Council's Planning Department, that the formal study of literature, or Great Books as she had put it in explanation to her complaining mother, would lead her to questions. She had hoped for information. For answers to her lack of it. For discovery of knowledge. And maybe, perhaps, enjoyment. All to be received, she had assumed, in dutiful and grateful silence. But Derek Holdsworth's ardent probing and his patent commitment to the life-changing properties of his subject had quite altered her perspective. Christine, as if a switch had been thrown, began to view her own life, its evasions and its end-stops, through the lens he had held up before them. It was not as clear as that for her all the time, and nor did she always see the connections, moral and life-enhancing he stressed,which she vaguely discerned were there to be made. Yet the questions were increasingly insistent, and troubling. Everything old was to be re-assessed. Everything new was to be tested. Every lazy assumption was to be quizzed. Every conclusion reached too easily was to be overturned. Her question, the one she had for him about Anna, was, she saw now, a question for, and so about, herself. It was an educated question.

* * * * *

Through the classroom windows Christine watched the students, the younger full-time ones, scampering past the gallery's incongruous Gothic bulk. So unsuitably dressed for this weather, she thought. The snow was falling still and making little crusts where it drifted into the corners of the windows. Christine thought to herself, with a small shudder of disdain, that no daughter of hers would ever have been allowed to dress like that in weather like this. No way. But then she thought that she might, no, would have had no control over the matter, would she. And that, besides, that her daughter, Grace she had called her, would have long since left university, if indeed she had ever gone. Surely, Christine mused, she would have done so. Surely.

Grace had been born at the turn of the New Year when her mother was seventeen. Christine had retired, with an adequate redundancy package on offer, when she was sixty, over a year ago and after forty years of service. Grace would be, and the number came up automatically as it had year on year, forty four years old. Christine had long since put an end to any impulse she might have had to cry on that birthday. The wrench which had occurred could not be undone.

Her mother and her father, though him less forcibly perhaps, had insisted it would have to happen. So it did. But, year by year, she worried away in her mind at the choices she had been made to confront. More ruefully the choice she had, was it in despite of herself, made. He had claimed his hands were tied but that he would support her in whatever choice she made. Abortion in a private clinic or a discreet adoption. Beyond that, Tony was not able to go. There was no other choice they told her. Mother. Father. Tony. Oh, Tony. Christine had known he was married but not, she swore, that he had two children under the age of ten. She had not meant for it to happen the way it did. "Ha," said her mother, "and even so, my girl, you can't claim to be innocent, can you? Just stupid."

Stupidity. A mess. What had she been thinking about. She had not been thinking at all, she said. Precisely, she was told. She must have led him on then. Need to be responsible. Stupid. Too young to have a baby. Too stupid to have a baby. To be a mother. And they, after all, could not be expected to take on another child. A baby. Not at their age. Christine had been made to contemplate, over and over, her stupidity. It only made her feel more stupid. Then, and since. Then, because she had been pulled and pushed into thinking herself selfish, and stupid, so she had, herself, actually chosen to let Grace go. Since, because she knew, even then, that she had indeed chosen. Not them. Her. Just as she had chosen to let Tony do what he wanted with her, despite her protests, because he, too, had wanted their love to happen. Or rather, since the love it seemed had only been on her side, their love-making. Sex, yes. But not, for her at least, only the sex. There had been passion. She had been suffused with it. She remembered all of it. Stupid, maybe. But passion, nonetheless, and without apparent limits to its power. Until it stopped, so abruptly, in deceit and despair. Then, as it played out and re-played in her memory over the years to come, she recognised it, or rather related it to herself, as something interchangeable, not unique at all. In its frame and in its detail it was of the kind of banality she would instantly register, identify with, in the novels she borrowed avidly from the public library. Always the same shelves, the same writers. Once outside the passion, just looking in, the cardboard cut-out characterisation and the cliché of Romance, stood in for the fate and the destiny passion had once promised her. A colleague had once flicked through a paperback she had been reading in her break. He was her age. He had been to university. He gave it back, with a smirk, and told her it was banal. She had looked up the meaning of 'banal' in the pocket dictionary she took to work. Its characteristics seemed to fit all her own circumstances all too well.

Girl leaves school at sixteen with modest but decent 'O' Levels. Girl joins local Council as a junior in the Planning Office. Girl lives at home with Father – a typesetter – and Mother – a housewife. Girl is tall(ish), for a girl. Girl is demure, awkward(ish). Girl is not pretty, plain(ish). Girl is uncertain, how not. Girl is young, and vital. So, untouched, unformed, open to life beyond her shelter, the girl is, naturally, enticingly attractive and utterly unaware. Enter older (just) man from adjacent office. He is not pushy, nor boisterous, nor overwhelming. He is neither a Lothario nor a Joker. Chance, apparently chance, encounters, over coffee, in the park at lunchtime, in the corridors, will and did, follow. Along with a spark, a scintilla, of friendship. This was Christine's new found friend, and adviser. This was, soon, to be Christine's first, and only, lover. Tony. He had a car. She lived on his way in to work. No need to catch a bus anymore. He would wait at the end of her street. Out of sight. Take her home, too. No problem. He was twenty-four. Married too young, he said. No kids, though, just the misery of a marriage to the mistake he'd made. Especially mistaken now that he'd met Christine who, whenever she thought back to the detail of her affair and of its consequences, shivered at how banal she had made her life. Until that is, she had read *Anna Karenina*. Oh, how instantly she understood Anna. Oh, how she feared for Anna. Oh, how she despised Anna. Oh, how Anna fascinated her.

In the classroom the ornate ribbed clunky radiators throbbed with heat, a mix of fuggy steam and metal paint. Christine took off her heavy, grey woollen coat and undid the knot with which she had tied her olive green, hand-knitted scarf around her neck. She smoothed down her black-and-red checked skirt and tugged her loose, beige pullover down into place. She scuffed her blue ankle-high wellington booties on the floor where they had dripped and made small puddles at her feet. The door opened from the corridor. Four others came in together and said "Good morning" and, in unison, stamped the snow off their Ugg boots. They sat down, behind Christine, and chatted to each other. Not to Christine. It was almost time. No others would come in this weather was the opinion voiced behind her. Christine opened the novel to the pages she had marked and wished to discuss. She went over the question she wished to ask. She had put it to herself in any number of ways. It would not come out quite in the way she wanted it to do , in the right and measured way, and she was stuck with it as it was, no matter how much she tried to move it around. The door opened again. Two latecomers joined them. Late by five minutes now. Traffic, they said. Chock-a-block in town. The snow. Delays everywhere. Perhaps the class would be cancelled. No one knew, or had had any message. Disappointed now, Christine moved her heavy shoulders, almost imperceptibly, in a kind of helpless shrug.

Outside the snow was coming down harder, thicker, in flurries, and it was sticking in granulated rifts spreading out from the recessed corners of the windows to the indentations made across the panes by the Victorian leaded bars which held the glass together. No undergraduate students could be seen any longer. The campus was all white by now and even the ugliness of its modern, blocky buildings was softened by their half-disappearance into the snowstorm. At 11.15 the class members, apart from Christine, began to shuffle their feet, finger the heavy coats they had draped over the back of their chairs , and begin to wonder if they should leave. The classroom door clattered hard against the wall. Derek Holdsworth had thrust it open with his left hand still on the handle and his right in the small of Diana Lewry's back as he held it open for her and ushered her inside. Snow flakes clung to them and they shook them off like dogs do, and laughed.

"Sorry, sorry, everyone," the Tutor said. The class nodded, and smiled forgiveness. "My damn car wouldn't even start, and I had to walk. No buses going down our hill at all. No gritters been out. Of course. This Council, eh? And thank God, at the bottom, Diana, Mrs Lewry, four-wheel-drive naturally for a Doctor's wife, spotted me and very kindly... well, here we are!"

The snowflakes scattered in Diana Lewry's hair were turning into jewelled melt – water droplets, silvery beads amongst black strands. She ran her fingers through her wet hair and flicked the strands to make them separate. She waved, an all-embracing wave, to the group. She unzipped a black, leather bomber-jacket with silvery zips and studs, worn over a cherry red angora sweater and a calf-length chocolate brown suede skirt, and she crossed her legs in her knee-length black boots as she sat, to the front, in the chair left for her by the others. Derek Holdsworth had watched the mini-performance even as he'd taken off his own duffel coat, wet and damp above the brown corduroy trousers and charcoal grey polo neck he had worn all through the winter. Somehow the sameness of it comforted the class in the same way Diana's colour and flamboyance added to their own pleasurable sense of being there, all of them, as a group.

Suddenly, within this tableau, without any expectation of understanding, Christine was taken by surprise. Pain, almost a physical pain coursed through her. It flooded in with no barriers of defence, no prior sense of its coming to forewarn her. Stupid. Christine looked up and across. At Diana and Derek. And she knew, all too soon and too clearly, that she was irretrievably stupid. Again. Of course. They're a pair, she thought. A couple. Lovers. She clutched her copy of the novel tight between both her hands. She stared, startled by her insight, the last to have it she now supposed, and she watched, dazed, as Derek Holdsworth unpacked his briefcase and scattered his notes, and all four of the novels to be studied, onto the table. He sat, motionless for a second, in front of his class and when he spoke, their attention all his, it was the pleasure of being there with them, again, which was audible in the tone of his voice, beyond the redundancy of words.

"Right, then," he said. "And of course with my thanks, ladies for your patience this morning. Well, here we are again, with our very own leading ladies before us once more." Derek Holdsworth touched each of the paperback novels on the table in turn and, one by one, held them up to show the covers. "Bovary ? Dead. Dorothea. Daunted, or was it dauntless. Did we agree? And the transparent, or is it enigmatic, Karenina to come, along with the whore, or is it the saintly, Nana. We will see, won't we? We will see."

Dr Holdsworth took another fifteen, well-honed and well-rehearsed minutes to offer them a resume of Tolstoy's narrative. He blended in the counterpoint story of the author's doppelganger, Levin, and rounded it off with a series of observations that came delicately couched as possible lines of enquiry. It was a skilful gutting of the plot and a helpful portal into its key themes. Dr Holdsworth gave his remarks the added frisson of both his professionalism and his scholarship by dropping in some arcane critical phraseology, and then concluded with a clap of his weather-reddened hands and a shouted cheery, "Voila!"

There was to follow, they knew, the silence he had induced in their collective response. Then he would smile encouragingly, and wait. The class, in turn, half-inclined as a body to see how and when, as usual, Diana Lewry would break ranks, grateful to her for being willing to be so forward. But the voice that came first this time was not that of Diana, in front and to his right but that of Christine on the side and to his left. She had, in truth, not expected her own voice to sound so harsh, the timbre so challenging, but she knew, of a sudden, that it was the unexpected tone of her voice which was, in fact, dictating the question. It came out in a rush and unprefaced by any preamble. "How could Anna just up and leave her son?" she asked.

Dr Holdsworth put on his bemused, but yet encouraging face. "You don't mean it quite like that, do you, Christine, uh, Miss Verity, do you?" he said, and went on, "I mean her motivation is reasonable beyond reason, is it not? The answer is love. The answer is lust. The answer is passion. The answer is Vronsky." A murmur of pleasure rippled through the group. Of course it was? How compelling was his answer. Yet not the answer Christine could accept. ? Miss Christine Verity answered in turn.

"No, Dr Holdsworth, uh Derek, that's not what I meant, your answer is to a different question. I mean, yes that's why she did it and that's why everything goes wrong for her. In the end. But it's always wrong, isn't it? And she knows it."

This time Derek Holdsworth decided he needed to take charge or else, he could see, they would never begin to unpick the novel – its structure, its multi-vocal effects, its radical use of stream of consciousness, its contextualisation of the 1870s, its critical reception, and all the wonders that came from this ur- text – in the manner he had envisaged, and needed.

"Look," he said, throwing a sidelong glance at Diana Lewry but leaning in friendly fashion towards Christine ("Ha! bloody verity – seeker," Diana had called her after one tortuous session on *Middlemarch*) "Look, Anna, a good and beautiful woman, in the throes of an uncontrollable feeling for Vronsky, with her loveless marriage to the desiccated bureaucrat Karenin, sees a door open into a life of sexual love, a Nirvana if you will, through which she must go. Now, admittedly, in that Russia, then, without an arranged divorce, one in which she must be presented, deceitfully of course, as the innocent party she will be ruined, socially and reputationally , to the point of complete exclusion from her class, from her friends, from society. That, as the tale unfolds will indeed be her tragedy. But, Christine, we must begin, mustn't we, in accepting the depiction of her…obsession, shall we say, with the adorable Vronsky?"

The word 'adorable' brought on some snickering of worldly knowledge amongst the group. "And now," said Dr Holdsworth, let's consider, someone please, the counterpointing narrative of Tolstoy's presence in the novel as Levin? Diana?"

Diana Lewry uncrossed her booted legs which the melted snow made shine beneath the fluorescent light. She raised a magenta coloured fingernail to her open mouth. The voice, though, was again that of Christine Verity.

"I see that, of course I do. That's still not my point, though. The point is, I'm saying, that to give in, as she does, almost from the beginning, is, well, wrong. And she knows it. Because Tolstoy knows it. And he never forgives her. She never forgives herself. It's why she throws herself under the train."

The tutor knew, in depth now, that there was only one way to deal with this rambling. He acted. "I don't want us to be led down this side path at the moment, Christine. I'm concerned, for the class, with the bigger picture. Let me spell it out for you again. Anna Karenina is de-socialised by her perfectly understandable actions, her love affair, with the sexually voracious and sexually magnetic Vronsky. Right? None of us would have any trouble with that in this day and age, right? But this unfortunate woman is, in a sense, denied her full humanity, her social being, because she follows her heart, and more than her heart, eh, to her destiny. Romance meets reality. Only one winner, there. That, Christine, is our kicking-off point, not the whole shebang , ok?"

Christine Verity sensed the group willing her now to let this go, to let the expertise of their teacher take them to a better place. Instead, she said, "That's still only description. I asked about her reasoning not her motivation. She had a choice, didn't she? It wasn't between her husband and her lover, it was between Vronsky and her son, Sergei Seryozha as she calls him. It's her son she abandons. And when all else goes wrong, too, it is that guilt which torments her."

Christine Verity opened her paperback to the passage she had marked in Chapter 23 of Part Two of *Anna Karenina*. She read it out aloud as if she was quoting a Biblical text, one she might have learned by heart. "What about this?" she asked the class, "Where Vronsky tries to persuade her to abandon her home, and succeeds. *So you really think I ought to run away and become your mistress do you?…become your mistress and ruin everything…she wanted to say "ruin my son" but could not bring herself to utter the words. Vronsky could not understand how she, with her strong and truthful nature, could endure this state of deceit, and not long to get out of it. But he did not suspect that the chief cause of it was the word—son, which she could not bring herself to pronounce. When she thought of her son, and his future attitude to his mother, who had abandoned his father, she felt such terror at what she had done, that she could not face it; but, like a woman, could only try to comfort herself with lying assurances that everything would remain as it always had been, and that it was possible to forget the fearful question of how it would be with her son.*

And then this, said Christine, and continued to read. *She could hear the sound of her son's voice coming towards them, and glancing swiftly round the terrace, she got up impulsively. Her eyes glowed with the fire he knew so well; with a rapid movement she raised her lovely hands, covered with rings, took his head, looked a long look into his face, and, putting up her face with smiling, parted lips, swiftly kissed his mouth and both eyes, and pushed him away. She would have gone, but he held her back.*

Christine closed her book.

"Yes?" said Derek Holdsworth. "This is indeed your point, I see. But it is the kiss, her kiss to him, that makes my point for me, isn't it?"

"It is what we are told. What we are made to see. It isn't, is it, what we are necessarily supposed to approve?" Christine said.

"Approved?" said her tutor. "Approved, Christine? We're getting a bit maiden-auntish now, aren't we? They can't keep their hands off each other, can they? That's the point, love."

Christine felt her mouth go dry. Outside the windows the snow was falling so steadily that nothing other than its falling and setting could be seen. In the classroom the students shuffled their feet, uncertain if the dialogue had come to an end. Given the way it was now being phrased, they hoped it had. It had not. Christine Verity could not stop now.

"They could have finished. Or Anna could have held fast, to the deceit. For her son's sake. Or Vronsky could, should, have restrained himself. For her sake," she said.

"Oh for Chrissake," Derek Holdsworth said with a tetchy exasperation. He had grown tired of this. "We can't moralise this away. Tolstoy is confronting us with the individual choices we sometimes make despite all of convention, all expectation, all consequences."

"No," said Christine. "Vronsky just wants to have her, that's all."

Diana Lewry laughed out loud. Derek Holdsworth smiled at her. "Ok, since you put it like that, I'll put it like this," he said. "Yeah, he wants to fuck her. Badly. Why do you think he wants to do that, Christine? He wouldn't want to fuck you would he?" This time Diana Lewry said, "Derek!" and he said, "Oh, sorry. Sorry" and opened his hands, palms up, to the class of women. The faculty wives smirked their forgiveness. They waited. It was Christine's turn, they knew. Christine Verity looked down at her own, large hands. She envisaged her face as he must see it, as her mirror showed it to her at home. Her down-turned mouth, her thin lips, her sharply pointed nose, her lank, graying hair. Even when she was young the mirror had never encouraged her. Only Tony had ever done that.

"No" she said at last. "You wouldn't either, would you. Not me. But, you know what Derek? The feeling is mutual. And I, I would always put the needs of a child before the selfish and the wilful." She stood up and gathered her things together. Her pens. Her books. Her notepad. She put on her coat and placed her things in a plastic shopping bag. She was sure she would not cry. Not yet. She turned her back on the tutor. She said, "And I'm going now. So goodbye everyone. And thank you,very much... for everything."

* * * * *

Christine Verity walked out of the gallery onto the snow-covered campus. No one followed her. She did not look back. The snow blew onto her face and melted into the tears blinked from her eyes. Snow and tears mingled inside her mouth and she swallowed their water. Her mouth was no longer dry. She walked alone and steadily over the snow to the bus stop. It was, at least, over for her and they could all think what they liked. Diana and Derek could do what they liked. She had said what she needed to say for herself. It was a form of atonement which reading Great Books had given her. There would be new steps to take. Christine considered, as she waited for the bus to take her to town, where she would shop for her mother's Tea, and what those next steps might be. First, there would indeed be her mother to sort out. She would finally then, she concluded do that. And maybe there were two or three letters to write. To Dr Lewry. To Mrs Holdsworth. Unsigned those, and typed. A handwritten one to the University's Vice Chancellor. That would be signed in blue ink.Not in the Great Books manual, she knew now, but then she had spent a lifetime reading other books. The banal had its uses, after all. And she would ask to be re-assigned to another class. She fancied "The Romantics: from Wordsworth to Keats" with Professor Idwal Jones (retd), B.A (Wales). Fewer letters after his name, and an older man clearly but with more in-depth maturity and substance perhaps. Christine decided she could, at least, picture 'Wales' more readily than 'Cantab' or 'Oxon'.

A pillar-box red Routemaster loomed up out of the whirling snow and pulled in at the kerb. Its doors sighed, and opened for her. Christine stepped gingerly up onto the bus and showed the driver her Senior

Citizen's free pass. She decided, unusually for her, to go upstairs. For a better view, she thought, as the bus lurched off, and why not. There was not much left, though, to see of the town spread haphazardly below and alongside the curve of the bay. Snow had blanketed all discernible shapes and was still relentlessly smothering the town from roof tops to gutters. Christine looked out of the window and, seeing nothing that was familiar, tensed with the sudden exhilaration of the righteous.

When the bus stopped outside the indoor market hall where she would buy savouries for tea at home, Christine was lost in her sense of well-being, and in the prospect of the well-doing that was to come in the Great Book that was now to be her life. It was with a start of alarm that she realised the sign for the market had been there, on the opposite side of the wide four lane road, for more than a minute, and that soon the bus would move off. She rose abruptly from her seat, her bag of books wobbling in her one-handed grasp as she grabbed the rail on the stairs and clambered down them. The driver, annoyed at her late decision, opened the doors for her and she half-fell onto the pavement where feet had already softened some of the snow into slush. Christine walked into the blowing snow towards the back-end of the bus as it pulled away, and she stepped out from behind it onto the road which she needed to cross to reach the market. In the blinding snow, she did not see, as it overtook the bus, the car which hit her with a force which was hard enough to send her sprawling up, over, and off its bonnet. Her head smacked onto the snow pillow of the road. Her neck was broken with the sound of a book's spine being cracked open. The falling snow, snow onto snow, muffled the terrible sound. Christine's books had been sent flying up from her flimsy bag as she dropped it. They half-opened themselves and fluttered in the air like ungainly birds before they fell to earth around her. Their pages flapped in the wind and the snow, and then began to curl up, wet and blurred, alongside her prone body as the blood trickled from her head and stained the snow on which she lay.

****

When the bus stopped outside the indoor market hall where she would buy savouries for teatime at home, Christine was lost in her new sense of well-being, and in the prospect of the well-doing that was to come in a life transformed by the Great Books which she knew she would continue to read. It was with a start of alarm that she realised the sign for the market had been there, on the opposite side of the wide four lane road, for more than a minute, and that soon the bus would move off. She rose abruptly from her seat, her bag of books wobbling in her one-handed grasp as she grabbed at the rail on the stairs and clambered down them. The driver, annoyed at her late decision, opened the doors for her and she half-fell onto the pavement where feet had already softened some of the snow into slush. Christine walked into the slanting snow towards the back-end of the bus as it pulled away, and she stepped out from behind it onto the road which she needed to cross to reach the entrance to the market. In the blinding fall of snow, she did not see ,until the last instant, a car overtaking the bus. Her arms jerked out in protest as her body half-turned, and her books flew up and out of her flimsy bag as the car squealed and skidded before it hit her. She fell backwards in a twist. First her shoulders and then the side of her head crumpled into the snow pillow of the road. Her books had fluttered,half-opened like the ungainly wings of stricken birds, and now lay around her on the ground, their pages soaked and their print blurred by the snow that had not stopped falling.

Christine felt someone lift her so that she could sit up. And someone else, the car driver perhaps, was saying over and over: "Are you all right, love? Are you all right? You just stepped out. I didn't see you. I couldn't see you, all the snow and that. The snow, see , love". Then there were more people around her. She heard other voices. She said she was fine, that it was Ok. And she thought to herself that she'd have to buy some more books to read now, wouldn't she.

PARTHIAN

He had not seen her since the night of the exhibition. He had not heard from her after Billy had left. She'd said, on the phone, that she'd just like to see him. To say hello, and see how things were. Oh, and she'd added casually, as Bran always did, to ask a favour of him. He didn't ask what kind of favour. With the ill-feeling and bickering, the malevolent quarrelling as the strike had finally unravelled, and then Billy's terrible success at the exhibition before Billy had said goodbye and left them all behind, including him, he felt he could not shut her, or her need of a favour, out of his life. Not without foreclosing on everything else. She wanted to come over straightaway. Half an hour by car from the city. They fixed a time for late morning, and she said that would be great, and see you.

He decided it was time to shave, to scrape off the bristly month-old half-beard. He shaved carefully, methodically, with scalding hot water from the kettle. He lathered the suds thickly with his brush and coated his face with them, more than once, successively removing them and the beard which they hid, doing it with deft sweeps of his safety razor until his face felt smooth again. He looked at its restored nakedness in the bathroom mirror. It felt to him like a discovery of self he did not want, but one he had been compelled to make, though he could not say why.

When he had showered and found one remaining clean shirt, still in its dry cleaner cellophane wrapping, he dressed in a black cashmere pullover and black cotton trousers. He looked at himself in a wardrobe mirror and decided, with a wry look at the creased puppet lines below his downturned mouth and at the folded-in jowls of his old man's neck, that, at seventy, he would have to do. He moved through the house then, though only downstairs, tidying things up, putting half-read books away, plumping cushions, gathering scattered newspapers together, taking rimed cups and stained saucers and empty plates into his kitchen, closing its door behind its mess.

He decided against laying and lighting a coal fire in the Victorian black-leaded grate which he and Billy had once found in the back garden of a deserted house in an abandoned street. It was the time when people had been moved out from the terraces in the valley bottom to be resettled on a new mountain-top housing estate, one that had slid into architectural decrepitude and social despair within another decade. The grate had been installed by father and son when they had knocked through from front-to-back in the forlorn seventies. Its surround of plum-coloured tiles, each with lime green tendrils garlanding their edges, tethered the stone-built terraced house, however incongruously now, to the detail of its past. Much like himself, was his unspoken thought whenever he looked at them. Against the dank November weather outside, he notched up the gas-fired central heating and made some real coffee in the gleaming Italian percolator Billy had once bought for him. He sat down before the empty grate to wait for his son's former partner to arrive. From the kitchen he could hear the sinister hiss and drip of the coffee percolating for them.

He began to consider what the favour she wanted might actually be. He dismissed the idea of money, since he didn't have any, and she wouldn't need any. Advice, then. At his age he was always being asked for that. He'd given too much of it, too recently, too brusquely, he thought ruefully, to want to go there again, especially not with her. Maybe information, then. He could understand her need for that. It was the same for him. Where Billy was? He didn't know. There had been no letters or cards or calls. What Billy had said, if anything, before he went? Nothing really. He'd muttered, "Time to move on", with not even a perfunctory hug to soften the declaration. The Old Man, as he knew and resented he was called, had shrugged at that and said – too sharply, was his later regret – that Billy had always been a time-and-motion merchant at heart. Click, click. Snap, snap. Take a picture. Any picture. Move on. So he'd said, "Yeah. Bugger off then", and picked up a book, wanting instantly to stifle the words and deny the sentiment. Too late both ways. He knew that much, but it was not for Bran to know, or care about. Nor had Billy left anything, words or objects, with him for her, and besides, they'd been apart for a while. So there was nothing there. He decided he didn't know what favour she could possibly want. When she arrived and he'd let her in and she'd kissed him on his cheek and sat down. She came straight out with it in that abrupt but disarming way she had. And he could not have anticipated it.

She wanted his life, she said. She wanted his memory. She asked him to tell her his whole story. She wanted to ask him questions. Or not, as she explained it, exactly that. It would be best, she said, if he could just free-flow. She'd smiled, self-deprecatingly, at the phrase. He'd grunted. It'd be easy, she'd assured him. Straight into a tape-recorder. She'd produced one from her bag. It was, and she waggled it between her fingers at him, the latest and most miniscule model. She told him she knew of his irritation with such things – his unease even, she'd heard him say, whenever he chose to pontificate to her generation – but, she stressed, this little beauty took the tech stuff out of the ology thing. Honest, she grinned. So easy, this one. Just switch on. Pause if you like. When you like. Batteries were long-lasting. Tapes, even these mini ones, did three hours each. There were more in tiny cellophane-wrapped packets. Simple to change them over. If he needed. And she placed the miniature instruments for his life's recall on the low deal table which stood, its original legs sawn down to coffee table height, between them.

Then they had sat together over the coffee he had made in his shining Italian percolator, that late November morning in the cold, ashen winter of 1985; and as he demurred, as politely but as firmly as he intended now that the favour had been asked, she countered his objections, his nothing-to-tell wave-of-the-hand dismissiveness, and began to make it personal in the manner she knew how to make count. For Bran. She wanted, she said, to draw him the bigger picture in which she was involved. It was such an opportunity. For her. It might allow her fledgling broadcasting career – and she made a winsome moue with her mouth – maybe, just maybe, to take off. A series. Thirteen thirty-minute episodes. For Radio Wales, with a possible migration to Radio Four if they caught the metropolitan ear. Nothing scripted as such. An edited montage of voices, only, to capture what lay behind the day-to-day events of the strike. Deeper currents. Social significance. Community spirit. She set each phrase before him like a market trader guaranteeing the goods. And his role was to provide a spine to what might otherwise be an unstructured cacophony of witnesses. She wanted, she said, the connection of experience. His knowledge. To show that defeat was not retreat but an engagement with survival by other means. She said the story she'd create was that of continuity in ordinary people's lives, from then to now, and beyond, as people being, despite themselves sometimes, still together. That would be her intended effect, she said. He listened in silence.

Billy, he noticed, had not been mentioned by her at all. Not once. Maybe, he thought, for the good. In the silence now dropping between them she said, more quietly and as a plea, that this was a really, really, big chance. For her. That she'd be the series producer. Not just a jobbing interviewer-cum-researcher. That the idea, for the whole thing, had come to her, the connective bit, because she'd been reading, at last, some of the history stuff he'd always been, and here she gave a little nod of her head towards him, "banging-on-about". Then Bran leaned over to touch Billy's father on his knee. Then she left her own chair to bend down, on her knees, before him. Her head was bowed, almost in his lap. Her hair had been cut since last they met at the exhibition. It was cropped very short, almost like a boy's haircut. Her black hair glistened like thick stalks of rain-stippled grass, and it smelled to him of citrus and strawberries. She lifted up her head to look at him, and said, "Please, Dai. For me. Billy would want you to, too, wouldn't he? Please." She rocked back a little, stood up and smiled down at him.

His son's name had been spoken by her at last. Her last, best card. He looked at her and wondered at her dogged persistence, at her determined sense of the justice needed to be done. In her interest. He did not know what to say. He shook his head. From side to side. Bran shrugged, but did not seem dismayed. She controlled the pace of the moment for as long as she wished. He took her all in now. Bran, in her current uniform. Riveted blue jeans tucked into low-cut black boots with dulled silver buckles for decoration. A short black woollen jacket, single breasted and worn over a plain white T-shirt. No make-up. No jewellery. No ring. No artifice. All plain dealing. With the future in mind. And so in need of a useable past. She sighed, but only slightly, as if he was being more of a disappointment to himself than he was to her, and as if, nonetheless, he deserved one last chance.

Bran tapped an unpainted fingernail on the tape recorder on the table before them. She slid the replacement tapes a little closer. She reached into the inside pocket of her cinched jacket and with a gesture so theatrical it might have been – perhaps was – rehearsed, she pulled out a sheet of paper she'd folded in two.

"I thought you might be a bit uncertain," she said. "So I took the liberty of drawing this up. To give you a clearer idea of what I mean. What's needed. For the programmes to be solid. To tell the truth. Like you can. Only you."

The paper, held still in her small and shapely hand, was a-tremble, as if it might, in itself, make the difference, fly into the gap between them and bridge it for her.

"It's a questionnaire", she said.

"I've typed it out. Others will have similar ones, but all bespoke, so to speak. Of course, you can go anywhere you like with it. In your answers. It's a kind of aide-memoire, I suppose. Or a prompt. I'd only edit."

She paused, thoughtful again.

"Look, we really need, you know, a real backbone, your story, for all the others we'd play in around it, because, you know, the longer haul, isn't it? You were in it, and also, you know about it, too, don't you? More than just being there. The history, I mean. You've taught about it. So, you see, I – we – have to have that spine. Your memory… of it all."

Bran had made her pitch. A good one, in the circumstances, she thought. Time to move on. She looked at the ugly, clunky, black plastic digital watch that smirked out its silent, undeniable presence on her wrist. She tapped it. Acknowledged it.

"It's eleven-thirty now", she said. "I'll come back after five. Tea-timeish. I'll bring a bottle, eh? We can toast absent friends, the one we both know, mm? Look, you old grump, you might even enjoy this. And don't worry about any hesitations or repetitions, I can always smooth all that kind of stuff away in the editing suite. Tell what only you know, eh?"

He wanted to say that knowing was one thing, but telling was something else altogether. And that any such knowing, which he could not deny, was not the same as the experience he could not discard. He wanted to say that time always stood still before it was gone, and that what came later as knowledge was, because it was from the past, only a future stuck in the groove of whatever was now. He said nothing, and she smiled as if his silence was a complicit contract made between them.

She said, "Look, got to rush. Back to work. Lovely seeing you again, Dai. Ta for the coffee. And all your help, of course. See you later, then. Okay?" And she put the questionnaire she'd prepared in advance onto the table set with the coffee cups and percolator. She said "Bye", with her back already turned, and let herself out of his terrace house as easily as she had just let herself back into his life.

* * * * *

WHAT I KNOW I CANNOT SAY

[For Dai Maddox
15 November 1985]

1. Tell us where and when you were born. And who your parents were.
2. What was your childhood, your upbringing, like?
3. How old were you when you left school, started work?
4. Tell us about work underground, in the pit.
5. So much happened to your generation in the thirties – hunger marches, strikes, riots, the Spanish Civil War – how were you personally affected, involved?
6. When and why did you leave the coalfield?
7. You went into the Army, didn't you? Tell about that and the War?
8. And after the War, what have we lost, have we gained anything? Did you?

Dai, say whatever you like, how you like, in your own words, you know.
Love
Bran
x

* * * * *

Holding the paper. Reading the paper. Staring blankly at the paper. Focussing. Wondering. Repeating the questions. Considering what it was. A road map. A menu. A list. What it meant. Meaningless, he thought. Not the way it happened. Or, yes, it was what happened, he granted. Might have happened, he supposed. Could have happened. To someone or other. To him, too. Suddenly short of breath. Wheezing through the latticed fretwork of his lungs. Dust. Not as bad as some. And cigarettes, yes, as he'd been told by more than one doctor. Which had, though long given up, made it worse. Emphysema. He could sense, more than feel, the gurgle in his chest, the urge to spit that was sucked back into a vacuum of dryness which made him gasp. A lack of air. Inside him.

Recovering. Looking again at the paper she'd left. For him to study. How to respond. What he knew, he truly knew, he could not say. What had occurred in his life, yes, some facts as might be said, if dates and names and things could be called such, but he could not say, he knew, what might still need saying if it was to be fully known, and not in this way ever, not directly. Speaking out loud, that is. Into a machine. To speak into that would only be to tell her what he might think she wanted, in her sense of the word, to know. And that would be far less than enough. For what he knew could not be said.

Yet, it could, perhaps, be told. If telling was what followed on from accepting the invitation to be questioned. All foretold, as it were, by being told already in advance, by the way in which a question elicits the nature of an answer. Or shapes the telling, at least. Guides the manner in which the tale must be told. Or worse, and he grimaced, shows how all is, by now, told. Gone and foregone, both. So, if so, why not tell all that will be nothing like it really was to live it? Rattle it off, then. His own story turned into a history fashioned for her needs. Rehearsal and enactment. Whichever came first. Whatever was which. This last, he didn't think, even now, he would ever know.

* * * * *

TELL US WHERE AND WHEN YOU WERE
BORN AND WHO YOUR PARENTS WERE.

Holy Innocents' Day. The 28th of December. In 1915. In a home for unmarried mothers in Cheltenham. Young girls, no doubt, from the country, from the coalfield, the town, the city. The war can't have helped. All those uniforms, and a break-down – no doubt, is there? – of some of the conventions of denial and disgrace. My father's name was absent from the birth certificate. I learned it later, though he was dead before the war's end and there was no outcome to our connection. I have left Billy some notes I made, and a letter of explanation. But none of that is for now. Not here. I know my mother's name, though I do not remember her. She left. And, in that sonorous phrase, "abandoned her child". Me. I was just two and a half years old at the time. Pointlessly, I've cursed her, or at least never forgiven her, all my life. My mother, Gwendolyn Ann. Gwennie Maddox. My name, on the certificate I later retrieved I mean, was put down by her as "David James Maddox". Her maiden name was my surname. My given name was David. Which I kept, though not the James part. Who was he? Her father? My father, I used to think. But it was not. Her occupation was put as "Housemaid". What could she do, you might say? More than she did, I'd say back.

I was, before I was three then, that summer of 1918 as the war kept on killing before it finally stopped that winter, put into the care of my Aunty Rose and her husband, Robert Holcombe.

* * * * *

WHAT WAS YOUR CHILDHOOD, YOUR UPBRINGING LIKE?

I was a child then, so I cannot say. I became something else, so I can remember, of course, but not make a judgment on it as to what it was like or its nature. I expect that others might say, from my recollections of it for them, that it was miserable, harsh, even cruel on occasion; limited, certainly.

Yet this is not how I recall it. I do that, how else? Day by day. Hour by hour. One incident or another. One sensation from that time to place against a thought about that time. I can only re-enter it, that time, when and how it lets me, and if I wish to go there.

There was, all year long, the foetid animal stink of the smallholding. Of pigs mostly. And rotting vegetation, animal fodder, shit. It seeped through the house, stone-and-brick-faced and detached. But the latter description is far too grand. It had been the workshop for the quarrying that cut the stone for the valley houses when the coal rush began in the valley below. It was two makeshift rooms, living and kitchen, end to end, and two small bedrooms, one on top of the other, at the end. The smell from outside sidled its way into our nostrils no matter how much snorting out of it you did, and it became a part of us, in our pores, our sweat, our clothes, our very sense of ourselves. In winter the stink was cold and sour, and the dark mud the pigs churned up in their pen was ridged stiff. It flaked or crumbled when you walked on it to slop out. In summer the mud, after rain, was creamy and grey, rippling in folds where the pigs rooted after the cabbage stumps we threw them. Often the three of us younger boys would, hungry ourselves, gnaw the stumps back to a white, leafless remnant. Rose and Bob had two sons five years older than me: the twins Dick and Jim, my cousins, with whom I played for a while. And there was Ivor, older again, and resentful of everything and everybody. I say it like that now – resentful – but perhaps it was not that which was felt, and not towards me as a child. More like an annoyance with my presence, one that could, and was, contorted into anger as we grew up together, sharing the same lumpy tick-mattress bed, with me at the bottom, with Ivor there too for a while, kicked and pushed by the twins. When the twins both went to work underground as collier boys, replacing Ivor who had left to marry in a hurry, and they had a shilling or two to contribute, as he had done, to the family purse, they seemed to want to make me feel, in my torment, their own rage. Punched and kicked, and thrown in, more than once, amongst the pigs, I would avoid the twins by day, if they worked nights, as much as I could, and hide away in the tightest, darkest corners of out-buildings even when my Aunty Rose called and called for me.

My mother's sister always seemed red and wet. She wore a pinafore each and every day as she scurried about, washing and boiling and cleaning what could never, what with mud and manure and black pats from the pit, along with its dirt, fetched in with the pit clothes, ever really be kept clean, though she tried. In the summer, or in the months of the lock-out after the general strike of 1926, I would take off into the fern-covered mountain slopes above the smallholding. Here was a rich loamy soil beneath the swathes of ferns which grew taller than a boy and spread unheeded in waving seas of fronds to hide me from sight. Green and upright as spears in summer, bronze and brittle when autumn came before winter laid them flat as bracken. But, again, though I can feel all that within me, I did not see it like that then; and I think it is only the way I came to draw and paint which makes me see it, now, in this way. It is imprinted in me, I suppose.

We had lived, when I first became an add-on as a part of the Holcombe family, down in the valley, in a three-up three-down mid-terraced house on the flat, in a street that curled away like a distended entrail from the pit where Bob worked and where we three boys would, in turn, follow him one day. After the three-month strike and shut-down for part-time working in 1921, Bob had had a bump underground. A roof-fall trapped him under its stone and shattered his left leg, so that he never walked without a limp after that. I think it broke him in other ways, too. And, for sure, after convalescence it was why, Bob being unable to resume work as a collier and not able to afford the rent, we moved out of the terraced house into the old quarry workshop buildings. He did his best to make a home of them, but it was never enough to stop the cold and the damp, and making a smallholding out of the yard and field only made it, for human living, worse. But before that, when we were still living amongst other people and I was not yet five, he bought me a flat tin of coloured pencils, of good quality I think, and a large pad of plain white paper. I had been ill that winter and a chesty cough that wracked my body had lingered on. He placed me on a chest in front of a back bedroom window that looked out onto the mountains and helped me choose the colours – sienna brown, forest green, bright vermilion, burnt orange, lemon yellow, dark and light blues, a matte black – that might help my marks on the paper scratch out a semblance of what I saw. He must have bought the paper and pencils with his meagre wages, or perhaps he had taken a few shillings from the allowance by postal order which came for me, I later learned, every month until I started work proper at fourteen. I whittled those first pencils down to a stump, found black-leads to replace them and some lined blue notepaper to work with, and always, after that, carried paper and pens or pencils with me. I think they became my voice. I had nobody who was my own age around me. Yes, at school, but I was no longer from the streets then, and no one came to the smallholding. What was below us seemed faint, grew distant, noises-off you might say, away from the whirr and grind of the pit's winding gear and the hollow, bronchial rasp of the colliery hooter. I was, in this sense, orphaned twice. Dogs were my company. We had mongrels, three or four at any one time, and none too friendly, though they tolerated me as I sought them out behind the corrugated zinc shed where Bob kept his tools and a few scrawny chickens who flapped and pecked to keep the dogs at bay and wary of them. So I was there, grudged and accepted, as an arrangement reached between sisters, though never explained to me since I was only the object of what had been settled between them.

* * * * *

HOW OLD WERE YOU WHEN YOU LEFT SCHOOL, STARTED WORK?

Did I ever leave school? Or, to put it the other way, how could I leave something to which I did not go? Except when forced. By authorities, though only intermittently, since they could scarcely afford the regular services of any "whippereen" to chase down such as me. By my aunty, I suppose, if she was pushed to do so. By teachers who may have recorded and reported any absences and marked me out, correctly enough, as sullen or wilful or difficult. I was certainly, whenever I went, silent. It was all happening outside whatever bubble of self-containment I had made for myself, and the learning was as rote as it was rudimentary, with hard hands striking out at will.

We were all poor, and I looked the poorest of all, from hand-me-down short trousers and pullovers with holes at elbow and sleeve to the cardboard in my shoe bottoms. Not, as I say, that I was alone in this, nor in the cramp and pain of hunger, in the general misery of those years. We were all held in the waiting room which was school until we could be discharged, basically equipped, into the common fate of our wretched lives. And, you know, I am sure that what passes here for the rhetorical flourish of an old man looking back is, and I assert it again, what we knew for ourselves to be the truth, even then, and even if we would not have known how to say it for what it was.

As for how old was I when I left, well – not thirteen, for sure, and still in the so-called Higher Elementary. I could read, though we had no books on the smallholding, and I could do my numbers, which is to say, work out how we never had enough pennies to turn them into shillings or silver to magic it into crinkly paper. One day, it would have been the summer, I just stopped going to school altogether and no one questioned it, and whatever went on in that red-brick and grey quarried-stone pen after that went on without me. Besides, by that time I had already been regularly out on the cart, sometimes day by day, with Bob, and had been so before the 1926 lock-out when everything that was bad for us all became worse.

Bob Holcombe did not work in the pits again after his accident.

Not underground anyway. He did some work on the surface. Moving drams about. Stacking timber. Tidying up the debris, the mess the pit shafts spew up. His injury, and I suspect the after-effect of the war, tested even his sinewy strength. I remember him digging in his allotment, pulling up potatoes and root vegetables to feed us. He would hang his old suit jacket on a post before he started to dig, but always kept a black waistcoat on, his shirt sleeves rolled up to the elbow, his hob-nailed, ankle-high boots caked in mud as he twisted and lifted the spade in that sodden soil. He wore a flat, dark cap on his head, whatever the weather. If I was watching he would grin and whistle, and pretend to tap dance on the earth until I laughed. I never called him "Uncle", only Bob. And I was "Davy" to him. Somehow when the horses were sent up from pit bottom – once a year, to feel the air on their hides, to blink, half-blind in the light, to rummage in the grass – he acquired one that had no pit work left in him. It was mangy looking, bare in places, and skittish. Bob found a cart, or rather, the plank-bed of one, and made shafts and a plank seat and greased the iron rims over the wooden spoked wheels. He sold a few things. He pawned his watch and Aunty Rose's so-called jewellery. Not her wedding ring. He bought bits and pieces for what he called his "Business". He contracted out to a small mineral water maker in the town. He harnessed the horse – it never had a name – to the shaft and he put me on the seat beside him, for his surly sons showed no interest, and a few days a week we would set out together on what he grandly called "his rounds". Like most things in my life, this, too, would end abruptly.

When we had first started, Bob and me, we had been up before dawn, even before the twins needed to get up to work – when there was work, that is – and Bob would rake the fire, coax some life into its ashes, with me half-awake, a slice of stale bread slathered in flecked grey dripping in one hand and a chipped white mug of weak tea in the other. But it was hot and sweet. We sipped from it alternately.

Then, outside in the half-light, with the street gas lamps fuzzy and ochre yellow in the valley below, he would lift me up on to the seat. He would already have harnessed the horse between the shafts; and with the reins hanging loose from Bob's hands across the horse's scabby back, he would click and clack his tongue to move it out of the yard onto the mountain path that led to a metalled side road, a leftover from quarrying days, which took us steeply down to the main road which ran from top to bottom of our valley, hemmed in on both sides by the snaking, tumbledown terraces which fell one on the other like dominoes laid out by a drunken hand. We would move on the main road at a brisk pace. Of course, there were no cars to speak of in those days, just a few horse-and-carts like ours and an infrequent bus, usually empty at that time. Every Friday we would travel five miles down to the mouth of the valley to the railway halt where passengers needed to change trains and where the goods train from England would stop on its way to Newport, a town we never visited. By prior arrangement, Bob would have four wooden boxes of fish thrown down to him onto the platform. The rest of our day would be spent riding up and down the perpendicular streets of our part of the valley to sell the fish. It felt to me a special thing to be doing, splintering open the boxes marked "Grimsby" or "Lowestoft" and levering off the lids to see the fish, still silvery and blue on their beds of packed and crushed ice, and feeling their cold, dead weight in the hand. Bob would fillet most of them, put the fish heads in a burlap sack to keep for the pigs, and leave a few fish whole. Hake was a favourite of the colliers' wives. And there was usually a cheaper box full of sardines, big ones, to sell whole. He would save some of these to fry for us as a tea-time treat at the day's end. Bob had open crates of pop on the cart to sell as well. The bottles would be bought and returned on a weekly basis. Those colours, made up with God knows what, would shine when the sun came up, and the light was filtered through their gassy liquid. Raspberryade was more pink than red, and Cherryade had a deep, glossy tint to it. There was white Lemonade and a bilious green Limeade, a syrup-of-figs brown Dandelion and Burdock, and a strangely glaucous, almost opaque, vanilla-flavoured Cream American Soda that was thought to speak for the good taste and refinement of those who bought it.

These bottles, from this local firm, did not have the more widely used elsewhere flip-up metal attachments whose rubber seals and china tops served to keep the pop stoppered in. Those who favoured this local brand preferred the heavy rubberised screw tops which let out the hiss of the fizz inside the bottle when you turned them between thumb and finger. I would knock on doors. Take the orders. Run back to the cart waiting in the middle of the street. Stand at Bob's side as he prepared the orders. And, with a square leather bag of coins strapped around my neck and hanging low to my waist, I would scamper to deliver the pop. I cannot describe the happiness we felt when we did all this, together. I cannot, of course, because it only resides, inert, in my memory. Saying it is not it at all. These details will not, I'm sure, be what you want me to say; these moments that surface indiscriminately, yet selected, too, because they are – have been left – in my head, when so much else, more important things, have gone. So why do I know, still, that exact sensation of holding the wet fish, slippery and glutinous, their scales flaking off but grippy, clingy amongst the melted ice in the bottom of their wooden boxes? The way they so quickly soaked their dank odour of seawater and death into the newspapers. The newspapers I had collected to scissor into squares the night before. Headlines, newsprint, those grainy news photos, all blurred and softened back into pulp.

When we were home, in front of a fire banked up all day with small coal, I would sit at Bob's feet to unpick from the backs of his hands and out of the cuticles of his fingernails the fish scales that had come to cover him when he slit open the fish to gut and fillet them. I would unglue a fantail of sticky, transparent platelets, papery souvenirs of a now useless armoury. The business enterprise such as it was could only survive in the reasonably good times. Our expeditions ended with the shrinkage of everything in the wake of the stoppages: the nine days of the general strike and the six months of the miners' lockout, in 1926. The pennies which had once been paid out for the small delights of fish and pop had dried up. No more fish came and, in the valley, soup kitchens flavoured their vats of hot water with diced vegetables and the bubbling scum from the fat of cheap cuts of neck and belly and offal which drifted in white skeins on the surface.

Our own pigs were killed, one by one. Bob did it himself. The chickens were long gone. I cannot tell you, other than by just stating it, how hunger gnawed at us, as if it was itself eating us to feed itself. Bob lay in bed most of the time. The twins brought home what they could, food or coal, scavenged from the town, or a sheep taken from a mountain farm at night and, once shorn, boiled in an old tin bath. They had lost the strength, or maybe the will, to bother me. I do not know how we lived through that autumn into the winter, though in the summer, the weather so hot that year, the hunger had been bearable, what with wild fruits and hedgerow leaves we called bread-and-cheese to pluck and eat, and what we could grow in the allotment to parcel out and to store.

Soon after the end of the lockout in November 1926, when I was nearly eleven, Bob took to his bed for good. No doctor was ever called. I'd say now that he just gave up, had had enough: the hopelessness of being hopeful. The horse went to the knacker's yard. Nobody missed it. The cart was dismantled, back to basics, but with the shafts still in place. It pitched backwards in the yard, up in the air. At first, I took to pulling it. I could not go all over, as far as Bob had taken us with the horse plodding up and down, but I knew the streets by then, and I had fully left school behind me. I missed Bob being with me, the first thing in my life I had ever known as something to be missed, and I cried to myself when, at first, I went out on my own, straining to pull between the shafts.

To make it easier for me the shafts were taken off by the twins under Bob's instructions, shortened and refitted at the back as handles so I could push the cart. What stock Bob had left, just small things now, were piled into cardboard boxes and stacked in the cart. Nothing was to cost above a penny. Small wooden reels entwined with cotton, white and black only. A cask of malt vinegar for pouring through a funnel into paper-plugged empty milk bottles. Cards of twined string. Packets of white lime. Rough hewn chunks of carbolic soap. And for all these things, with buttons and marbles going for only farthings and ha'pennies, I was given big round brown pennies with Edward or George, or even Victoria, rubbed smooth on the front and with Britannia still raised in slight relief on the back with the embossed date to stare at. Very rarely an occasional silver thruppeny bit glinted amongst the copper which stank my hands as I shuffled it in its thin layers at the bottom of my leather bag.

I gave the money to Aunty Rose as Bob told me to do. Once, he sat up in his bed when I came back from tramping the streets, and said he wanted to give me something. He took an old biscuit tin out of the drawer of a rickety bedside table and removed the red-and-gold embossed lid. He smiled at me and said to look at this. In his hand he held out a flat piece of dull slag about two inches thick and six inches long. The slag was in two separate pieces. Bob took the top layer off. On the bottom half, protected by its own lid, was the shiny, black and indented impression of a fern. No, not an impression. The real thing, compressed and flattened, but transfigured so that its fine tracery of leaf and stem was splayed out in all its delicacy. It was still of the swamp forest from which it came before streams and silt had deposited the successive layers which were to be folded and crushed and buckled into the coal seams which later brought us all to this place. And now, all of us, fossils from another time. Bob said it was the finest example of a proper fern he'd ever found or seen underground. He'd kept it with him through the war, wrapped in cloth in his knapsack. A charm. A keepsake. A reminder. He wanted me to have it. I treasured it and took it away when I, too, went.

When Bob died, not long after this and just before the spring came, I kept the cart and managed the rounds for a while, until there was nothing left to sell to those who could scarcely find pennies any more with which to buy anything. Then a wholesale butcher in the valley took me on as an errand boy. I was fed, not paid, doing whatever a boy could do. I slept above the slaughterhouse. No one on the smallholding had tried to detain or dissuade me. But in the valley I was alone, an outsider, and for a long time this would be the mark of my life.

* * * * *

TELL US ABOUT WORK
UNDERGROUND, IN THE PIT.

There are few left who could do that. Few of us left who once worked as miners before mechanisation, before conveyor belts and power-loading and steel supports for the roof and pithead baths. Pit props notched and put in place by master craftsmen who could hear a creak and know whether to flee or trust their handiwork. Coal that was worked by mandrel and shovel by men who could read the coal seams for the habits and inclination of that hard-won mineral. Drams that were expertly raced with lump coal to make them as full and laden as possible. And a lexicon of technical terms and a glossary of slang to trick it all out as a lost, secret world. You see, Bran, where I could be going here, don't you? And I won't, or can't, play that game, make us more glamorous and less ordinary, and not just what we were, who we were, condemned to do what we did, with only a few fools luxuriating, for a short time of youth and health, in the vigour of what they did. But it is not a kind of Meccano set to recall the wing nuts and bolts and flat-headed screws, and the ingenuity of what was done. It was, in fact, a kind of hell, one made all the more so by its being literally below the earth's surface, and it killed you, piece by piece, or in an instant, and there was no let-up to the demands it made on both mind and body. The awful thing, of course, was that in the early thirties we yearned for it. Work, I mean. For there were no wages or a living any way half-decent without it.

Through the twins, both colliers when they could be, I was taken on, though not by them; and at fourteen, as a collier boy, apprenticed, you might say, to one veteran collier or another, and gratefully so. I was always set to work for those with no relatives of their own, so simpler to exploit. A few shillings were thrown your way sometimes. Our trumps. You learned by watching and by serving, as a slave, and what solidarity there was touted about, then and later, was never extended to the relationship between us and some of the bastards who worked us, their collier boys.

Work underground, too, was never a uniform thing. Pits could, and did, vary as much as the seams that lay, variously, within them. There were wet pits where the water seeped and dropped, cold and constant, from the propped-up roofs to fill the roadways and stalls with deep, coal-slurried puddles through which you sloshed or in which you lay to cut the coal. There were dry pits where the moisture-less heat was such that, even in winter, you worked side by side, in singlets soaked so wet by your sweat that they stuck tight, black and prickly to your skin. All the coal I ever worked before the war had to be hand-cut and hand-got, and some had to be chiselled out from seams so low you had to crawl in and out underneath them with, often, a powder charge to dislodge the pressure, and then use muscle to pull it down in great, shuddering ledges and lumps as big as boulders which fissured open and glinted with their hidden light as our lamps picked it up even in the blanket darkness of underground.

So-called normal conditions, varied and unpredictable as they were, were not the worst of it – nor was the danger from a collapsed roof or a rush of water from old headings, nor a fire-damp explosion. Things with which we all lived, necessarily insensible to it all the time we worked. But the true killing factor was the incessant, unchangeable, unremitting sameness of it all, from first light to pallid afternoons, or from nightfall to a crystal dawn that you shunned for bed. Relentless fatigue. Bodies running on empty. Minds drained. Exhaustion that no respite of sleep, of food, of drink, of any snatched pleasure, from sport to sex, could ever alleviate. It was a way of being tired, and working on despite it. That was a way of life. I felt for the first few years I worked as a collier boy that I would never face anything worse. Not even as a fully fledged collier myself.

I would be wrong about that, too. But I was only fourteen, remember, when I first knew the wrist-breaking weight of a curling-box. That was real, and terrible to me. Curling boxes, wide and flat metal baskets with a downward curved lip at one end, used by collier boys to scoop up the coal pick-axed to the floor of narrow seams, anywhere from eighteen inches to two and a half feet high, by colliers lying on their sides, bellies distended, backs arched and forearms punching. Then the curling box slid in and under to be filled with the cut coal, up to half a hundredweight at a time, pulled out by extended arms and backs bent to strain with the weight and the angle before being shifted into a waiting dram, the smaller coal in-filled between the walls of lump. Hefted. Placed. Piled-up. Trimmed. A skillfully raced dram to be check-weighed. A boy's extras, his trumps, could come from how well he judged the loading of his dram.

There would be fine clouds of coal dust hanging and floating in suspension, filling the air, clogging it with their soft, pillowy swirls. Black particles of coal dust, big enough to be seen, some of them, as singular motes that could gather inside your nostrils, or smaller ones to cake your eyelids and thicken your eyelashes as if by grotesque mascaraed make-up which only Vaseline could later remove. Your tongue and your throat would parch and dry, with just a swig of tepid water from your tin jack at snap time to offer relief and to wash your lips, before a sandwich of bread and cheese and raw onion would be taken from its grimy, greaseproof paper and held up away from the squeal of the rats you learned to kick away with your hob-nailed boots. Thumb prints made black dents on the bread. There was always a rank smell beneath the earth, a compound of reused air streams and the whiff of the rotted plant matter that was, after all, the coal itself. The stink of our own shit, shift after shift, lay stagnant in the still air, wafted to us from the holes off the main roadways where we would squat to relieve ourselves. No cigarettes, of course, to ease the throat and fool dust-lined lungs, just plugs of tobacco sliced off with a knife between finger and thumb to chew until its juiciness of cured leaf could be gobbed out as a viscous stream of yellow-flecked spit.

When the coal could not be extracted with ease we would be working to remove the accumulated mounds of muck and slurry, the heaped up scatter of stone and rubble which came down with the coal, especially when shot-firing had been used to advance the heading we were working. You'd skin your knuckles if you took your eyes off the rocks being thrown at you to clear the work space. Hang-nails or blackened ones set to die later were common, day by day, and the cuts and bruises that marked hands and chests and faces would stay as livid pockmarks, the blue scars that were the etched-in lines of coal which flesh folded itself over to trap beneath our skin.

I broke fingers in both hands in this way. But unlike others I saw I had no broken or, worse, shattered limbs or a broken back, a splintered face, a crushed skull. Death left me alone even if life would not, claiming others, men who had to be carried out of the places at the coal face to which hours before they had walked and crawled and stumbled. Weariness does not even touch it, since we were not tired to the bone, as the empty saying goes; we were hollowed out with tiredness deep inside, as if our own seams of being were being mined. You can see why it can never be forgotten by those of us who endured it day by day, to be fed and watered and washed day by day, to be sent back, day by day. But remembering it, truly remembering it, is not, though I can put it no other way, in the detail of it – not really. It is in the beat, in the pulse of its memory, unbidden and unwanted in your blood.

* * * * *

SO MUCH HAPPENED TO YOUR GENERATION
IN THE THIRTIES… HUNGER MARCHES, STAY
DOWN STRIKES, THE SPANISH CIVIL WAR…
HOW WERE YOU AFFECTED PERSONALLY?

Look, these things are markers you've picked up from books. Categories of a general life… Boxes which opened and closed, for some. Maybe other lives, older than mine or better informed, were held by them… contained by them. But not mine. Remember, Bran, I was only twenty in the middle of the thirties, and the coalfield was a mess after '26. There was no organisation after that. I wasn't a member of the union, the Fed, but then most people weren't unless they held a Show Cards on the pithead to shame men into joining. Whatever fight back came was one that came after my time underground. I left when it properly began, with the stay-downs of 1935. Hunger was just a groaning stomach for me. Not a march. Whatever was beyond just getting by, I let pass over me. I had no family. No dependents. I drank with some butties, but no friends had grown up with me. I lodged, paid the rent, mostly in the home of an older, unemployable collier. When the strikes broke out – orchestrated, more like – I saw no reason not to work, paid no subs or dues and had not a political thought in my head. I could have been one of those who strolled down the street, flanked by policemen no bigger than battleships, howled at by pinafored women banging on kettles and drums, to earn my pittance. As a blackleg. A scab. It would not have troubled my conscience. I wasn't yet twenty. I was alive with a vitality that was indifferent to what now figures for a common morality in history books. And, inasmuch as I had a motive to act one way or the other, it was having no ties and being otherwise adrift that inclined me to leave rather than fight on anyone's side other than my own. It was all a blank for me, I promise you. And, you know, I would say that it was the same experience for most, except then made different, necessarily so, for those who had no choice but to stay.

* * * * *

WHEN, AND WHY, DID YOU
LEAVE THE COALFIELD?

That was when I left. As to exactly why, well; as I say, an explanation is not the same as a reason, though maybe I had no reason as such – only appetites, which I fed. In what I can only call a glimpse of a better life. Better in the feeding-me sense of it, that is. There were new arterial by-pass roads being built across England, more in the South East and the Midlands than elsewhere. And factories being built for cars and other things we would seek to buy, all of us, later – wouldn't we though? – but then, oddly and perversely enough, not by me.

So, yes, I laboured. I tramped. I worked on building sites, in farms and in factories. I slept in doss houses. I slept rough. I shovelled whatever shit needed shovelling.

My personal life had no, what shall I call it, grain to it. There were some girls, of course, and pictures and booze, but it was as abrupt and mechanical as eating and breathing. I will not trouble you with it, or myself with the pointlessness of it. I had escaped, was how I saw it.

Other than for the one thing which had gripped me. I mean that I began to read. With no pattern to it, but without cease. Perhaps it was being in the warm, in public libraries. Maybe time to kill in the day. Anyway, I read anything, and everything. When my vocabulary petered out, I bought a pocket dictionary. I pondered new words. I puzzled over "paradox" and "ramifications", over and over, I remember, in a way that has stuck . What they meant. Was it because I was living a paradox and it had its own ramifications? Yet your questions seek a sense of order where there was only chaos. I repeat that I had no expectations or direction in my life. What there was of hope and desire went into the drawings I still did – crudely, of course – and, secretly, into the colours I began to use beyond the lines. I think, though without my consciously knowing it, that the reading informed that, too.

And then the war came, and the Army enrolled me as effortlessly as all else had swallowed me whole.

* * * * *

YOU WENT INTO THE ARMY, DIDN'T YOU?
TELL ABOUT THAT, AND THE WAR.

What I remember if, as now, I try again, is the routine of it: the repetitive training, the risible commands, the stretches of boredom, and then an added compound of the unknown, of an almost unbearable sense of scale, of men and distances, of removal to unthinkable desert spaces and sirocco winds full of sand which speckled your lips and clogged your nostrils. The terrifying, blind urgency of combat. No, more the way fear was displaced by killing, or being killed; or, if not displaced, somehow held in reserve until the time for terror returned, as you knew it would after North Africa and then into Sicily. Also, unwanted but physical, there is a reminder I cannot, living where we live, avoid. Rain. Cold. Dripping. Bone-chilling rain. Soaking through battle dress and oilskins both. Rain for weeks on end. The freezing, wet winter of 1943, and on and on into 1944. In sunny fuckin' Italy. That's what we all called it, and meant freeze-your-bollocks-off Italy. Before our lot went in at Cassino we waited, day by day, for three weeks; each morning stood down, waiting for the weather to lift so the bombs could be dropped. Each day not a torment, mind you. Just a pain. Get on with it, we all thought. And we said, "Send Bradman in to bat." That was the trigger code dreamt up by some clown at HQ. Because it was New-Zealanders, Maoris mostly, who were to spearhead it all. And that clown didn't know Bradman was an Aussie. Pissed the Kiwis off no end. So they waited, too, along with Gurkhas, Indians and our own Desert Rats. Me included. The latest to have a crack at Cassino, that small, nondescript cross-roads town, a stopping-off place for those going south to Naples or north to Rome. We were going north. Or trying to. Up Route Six. Up the Liri Valley that curved around Cassino to the left and arrived like an arrow into the Eternal city. If we broke through, that is. And then the Allied troops who landed further north at the Anzio beachhead, all sand dunes, sunken ravines and swamps, pinned down for months by German artillery and dog-eat-dog raids, could themselves push on. End of the war in sunny fuckin' Italy.

Only at Cassino there was a mountain, high, straight up, looming over the town and with a Benedictine monastery stuck on the summit, commanding the entire terrain and fully garrisoned. Around it or inside it were – a moot point – crack paratroopers. As an observation post it was an artilleryman's dream, and for the infantry set to take it, a nightmare.

They just couldn't take that hill or its monastery. No matter how hard they tried. Troops sown all over the slopes in rocky defiles and hidden gullies. For months. Assaults, frontal and sidelong, attritional and full-on, all failed. Finally, in February 1944, they bombed the shit out of it. Destroyed it. The Abbot and monks had been warned and were evacuated, taking their treasures with them. The town had already been bombed. A ruin for a long time. The Germans had moved into it. And into the ruins of the monastery, for sure.

In the middle of March we were pulled in, around the town, on the adjacent hills, strung along ridges, bivouacked near the river at the plain, and readied for what would be the third – and the last, we hoped – Battle for Cassino. If only the rain would stop. Had to stop if the bombers were to do their stuff. To flatten outright the entire town or whatever in uniform lived, breathed, shat and lurked within it. Then, on a Wednesday morning, the rain finally stopped. The planes came. They came in waves for an hour. When they left all was different, and nothing changed. As yet. Nothing is false in this account of mine. But everything is wrong. It is like looking on back at it as we looked at it then, but then was different. Not because we were waiting our turn to die and that the fear of it was a real taste. A taste of what, I do not know – some secretion of bile I suppose, not felt or tasted since, anyway. More because – my disdain for the recollection, I mean, and it is this I want you to see, if not to comprehend – it wasn't me that it was happening to, because none of us were us any more, not as we had once been. We had become other. You had to if you were to survive. Bodily, yes, we survived, not simply by avoiding madness by all kinds of pretence of normality – sharing whatever we had, from jokes to letters and news – but by being other. I am saying that we who had seen what we had seen and done what we had done were no longer the same, what we once were, what we wished to be again; and, believe me, we never would be. I knew I was a killer and they could justify it, as could I. Yet I was not; it was this other who did these things and wished that Wednesday morning for more killing to be done – much more – and not caring if it ended, whatever that end now was, since none of it could end until I could come back. As myself. And besides, in Cassino town, there were no civilians left. Only Germans. Nazis. The enemy. To hell with their names, their faces, their pasts. Let them have no future after the bombs fell. But they did.

In the town, there would still be Germans. When we went in at last. Dug in. Pillboxed. Tunnelled under. All this in the ruins of what had been the centre of the town. Reinforced positions, encased by concrete, in what had been palazzos and hotels. Tanks sunk deep up to their hulls in lobbies and hallways. Not destroyed at all. Waiting for us, to beat us off as they had done those like us before us, for months on end in the cold and the rain, from the winding river to the battered town, from the marshes of the sodden plain to the hairpin vertical roads twisting and corkscrewing through the scrub and the rock to the monastery still waiting to fall, the constant sight and menace above everything.

The monastery was just visible to us as we waited in our lines. Its remains still looked down above the dust and wind-borne debris rising from the final destruction of the town. It already seemed to matter less than it had to us fools who believed that what had been promised had been delivered, handed to us on a plate, the plate of the little smashed-up town just to our north. The flattened and obliterated town.

Below the ruin of the monastery and three hundred feet above the town itself was the site of an earlier ruin, a medieval fort on the knoll of Castle Hill. It was a salient, a station, a jumping-off point which we were to capture like the town itself, all before the last push on up to the monastery. We all knew the drill and as the bombs stopped, precisely at noon, and the final softening-up artillery barrage commenced, our tanks began to fire up, to rumble into the ruins with us, the infantry, to follow in their unstoppable wake.

Tactics had been spelled out. To fulfill their oh-so-fool-proof strategy. Objectives in the town to take and to hold. The sweep through the lower town to the railway station, then beyond, out onto Route Six and the plain opening out to the north to Rome. Castle Hill secured and held; then troops to go further up in the lee of the monastery, overwhelming the shell-shocked defenders. Victory.

Tactics that would be a piece of cake to carry out. Almost nothing and nobody could have survived the destruction that we had seen rained down on them for an hour. That is what we had been told. It was what we believed – what we wanted to believe, anyway, when low-flying bombers kept winging in and releasing their loads, shitting flame and explosives as we cheered. It would be a mop-up operation. Unstoppable tanks. Indomitable infantry. All objectives reached and secured by late afternoon. Yeah, sure.

But by nightfall it rained again and there was no moonlight to guide us amongst the jumbled landscape of wreckage and ruins where we had fought all afternoon for footholds, not strongholds, against an enemy who had risen up to meet us. An enemy who still existed. A hidden enemy, an unseen enemy, who had emerged, pocket by pocket as our tanks and troops entered into their line of fire, set up to slaughter us. From the redoubts they had made of cellars. From the shelling platforms they had disguised and protected within the recesses of the thick-walled stone dwellings and buildings of Cassino. Coming out, in ones and twos and platoons, from a network of tunnels. From crannies of rock reinforced with roofs and walls and set amongst the stony granite paths of the hillsides. Amidst the mound of hillocks of rubble, from blasted-out window embrasures and from doorways without doors, from behind piled-up masonry and iron and steel, as snipers, deadly and fleeting. With hand-held rocket launchers and hand grenades, machine guns and rifles, and with shells directed from the monastery, they killed us at will. Our tactics were dead for us even before they could be employed. The bastards had survived, able still to defend against us in what had become a defender's playground.

I read, after the war, that some Germans who had been at both thought it was worse, in the closeness of the fight and the quickness of the killing, than Stalingrad. Some older men amongst us said it was like the Somme had been in the First World War. And the tanks, sent in to clear the way for us, were of no use, ruled out of the action by the vast craters the falling bombs had made. Craters so wide and so deep the tanks could not bridge them and fell into them, got stuck in them. Craters so large and so yawning that soldiers could only go forward by scrambling, hand over foot, into the holes and then having to pull each other, hand over hand, out of them on the other side whilst the stalled tanks, their engines choking or brewing up from direct hits by hand-held *Panzerfaust* wielders, only helped to block the planned and rapid advance of the Kiwis through the town.

The craters filled with water as the rain came down again and became matte black pools to drown in. Maps and photographs of the town as it had been were useless in the rubble of streets collapsed before us. No landmarks recognisable. No street signs that pointed to any direction we needed to go. We guessed. We floundered. We were lost. There was no front line behind which to regroup and be steady. Killing, by us of them, was done from house to house. Pin grenades in to be met by stick grenades from them, and mad dash rushes across a scythe of machine gun firing. Boys falling. Any concerted attack was cut up. All was stop-start. In some buildings we entered we shared adjoining rooms with an enemy or we swapped positions floor by floor, and always so close you could see the men you killed or who killed you and heard the screams. Better be dead than what happened to some boys, and death was random in this killing place. Splintered wood or ricocheted stone could kill as indifferently as an aimed bullet or as all-embracingly as a mortar shell exploding amongst a surprised few. This, I tell you, cannot be imagined. Not by you now. Not even by me then. It was not, in the sense of knowing it as it happened, anything able to be experienced. It could only be endured. Only endured. As if it had no end to it. As if it was the only real thing. As if it was the end of the world itself. As if day by day and night by night, it was whatever life had become, with no exit, other than madness or death.

All this happened in the third Battle for Monte Cassino for over a week in March 1944 in sunny fuckin' Italy, until – nothing more to be done, slogged out by fatigue, some whole units crushed, beyond any conceivable objective being secured other than the holding of little bastions here and there in the town and up to the monastery on Castle Hill – with no breakthrough achieved, there was withdrawal, and the waiting all over again. It was called off and we left our dead, and their dead, amongst the ruins and we fell back. You asked and I have answered, and yet I have not said anything that is near to it as it happened then, and the rest is, ever since, a dream.

* * * * *

He lay flat out on his stomach with his back bared to the sun which was directly overhead above the stone-flagged yard in sunny fuckin' Italy. Now, in late summer, it was indeed and at last sunny fuckin' Italy, so they had taken off their webbing, their boots and their battledress blouses along with their coarse khaki shirts, and they lay, most of them, drunk and naked except for their trousers in the noon heat of the fuckin' Italian sun. There were twenty or so of them, and no officers amongst them this afternoon. They had been on patrol in the morning, clearing a small town that was empty of threat.

This was just to the north of Turin. And on the outskirts of the town, dull and industrial on its flat plain, was a distillery that made vermouth. They decided, on the instant, to liberate it, and to rest up. The air was a-shimmer in the heat and heady with the cloying aroma of alcohol, herbs and spice. No one had drunk this stuff before, neither the bianco or the rosso, though they had swilled gallons of the south's roughest red wine and burned their throats with tumblers of grappa. Pissed. Arseholed. Fighting. Killing. All their way up the fuckin' Italian peninsula. In rain. Through mud and snow. Across rivers. Over mountains. Down roads. Downhill all the way now. All lines breached. The partisans out and about. Bodies strung up. Women's heads shaved. Germans gone.

They whooped when they smashed open the heavy, hinged wooden doors to the courtyard and saw the rows of casks, huge oak barrels bound with iron hoops and stacked on their sides down three high crumbly brick walls. They used their rifle butts and their trenching tools to knock the bungs out of the barrels. The liquor spilled out onto the floor. They caught its pouring in their metal water bottles. They glugged the liquor, sweet and pungent, and cursed it for the shit it was, and drank it anyway.

The courtyard was open to the sky. Its floor soaked up the liquor. The stone became tacky with the stickiness of the sugary liquid. The liquor seeped into corners and blistered in the sun. It pooled itself into glistening drops, small rainbowed puddles of it, between the rough flagstones and the bumpy cobbles. They lay, insensible, amongst the gift they had been given.

In the middle of the courtyard were three industrial-size steel vats, about twenty feet high and ten feet across their oval shaped perimeters at the top. Fixed steel-runged ladders were etched onto their sides. He watched idly through one half-opened eye as some men started to pull themselves up the ladders, arm over unsteady arm, and then lurched, laughing, over the top into the vats. Splashing. Swimming. Sucking each other under in the fermenting liquor. More alcohol. Rawer alcohol, cooking away in the razzle dazzle sunshine beneath the open blue sky.

More soldiers began to career about, hopping and falling around on the courtyard floor, some grabbing their oblong mess tins, pushing each other onto the sketchy ladders. He saw that little runt, Nipper, at the bottom, not going up, holding his left leg with his hand, shouting others on. He saw Lofty, slapping Nipper aside, on one leg, pulling his trousers off, scrambling, hooting, cursing, onto a ladder and climbing up. He stood perched on his toes on the rim of the middle vat, opened his thin-lipped mouth wide and kept it open as he screamed and went head first into the vat. He heard him splashing about and shouting and gurgling in the bruising heat of the early afternoon's sun.

He turned over, onto his side, and in the buttoned-down pocket of his blouse he found a hand-stitched wallet of soft brown calf skin. A souvenir, along with the memories he preferred to discard, of a week's leave in a Naples, as degraded as he was by war. He took from the wallet the folded newspaper photographs he had cut out. He flattened the creases, smoothing the blurred images, his fingers gently passing over the past. One showed a wispy blossom of smoke, shell fire between the monastery and Castle Hill, almost like an apologetic cough as a calling card in January. The other, on a wider front, was of the firestorm that had been rained down on Cassino town at midday on 15 March 1944. The destructive hammer blow, the captions declared, that was to open the path to Nazi capitulation and Allied victory at Monte Cassino. He touched, with the index finger of his right hand, the black, mishapen form of Castle Hill, and he ran it down the direction they had taken that final night, back down to the town, down to the Hotel Continental to liaise with the Kiwi troops who would have taken that strong point. The Lieutenant had picked him out along with four others to form the platoon. To report how they'd thrown off the enemy, hand to hand, grenade by grenade, bullet to bayonet, from the walls of the medieval ruins as the Krauts had counter-attacked from higher up the hill, coming on them in waves until there were no more of them to come, and so how Castle Hill was being held, still, as a jumping-off point to the monastery. But the safety of the Hotel Continental would be no safety at all, and the monastery would not fall.

He lay on his back and looked directly at the sun, and he closed his eyes, blinking and dazzled by the sun. Black spots and bursts of red lit up the screen of his shuttered eyelids and served as semaphore for memory. Not as the recall of any felt sensation, one to be transfixed once focussed in the mind. Instead this was memory as a known shaping of what had once happened. To him and to others. The creation of memory as a structure to let him move on, move away, act as the survivor he knew himself to be. A survivor. One of three out of six who had followed the officer out of the keep of Castle Hill over its rubble and into the darkness. Orders. Reconnaissance. Radio communication gone. Connecting and communicating. Onto the twisting bends of a path overhung by boulders and scree and overlooked – but where, and how? – by the recoiled enemy, half a mile precipitously down to the town. They passed other troops – Indian Army mostly – bivouacking under rock overhangs out of line of fire, and they took in the grim warnings they were issued as they pushed on, stumbling, on the trail, cutting their hands on splintered rock, gashing their knees, as silent as they could be in the darkness that wrapped them and concealed others in ambush for them.

Now, in the sun outside Turin, he lay still. A survivor. One of three from that platoon. He looked again at his crumpled newsprint photographs. When he was in that battle – the third as they said later, with the fourth and final one in May to come, with yet more dead for whatever the victory was meant to be by then – he had known nothing, and thought even less, of what Cassino itself was. He had read more about it since, after he had been taken off the line and put in reserve for the breakthrough to the north. It was the

41

officer he had propped up against a sofa inside the Hotel Continental who had begun to tell him. He had given the officer a shot of morphine against the pain of his smashed leg. A cigarette was stuck, smouldering, to his lower lip. His eyes were dilated, black, and depthless. He kept saying his name was Cleave, Lieutenant Timothy Stafford Cleave, Royal Kents. To tell his parents, please. If he was to die. Couldn't remember the address. He had laughed at that, giggled. He'd said the College would know. To tell them, and they'd send the message on. To his parents. The college was Caius – he'd spelled it out for him – in Cambridge.

This was all while they huddled in a room, its floor a carpet of chandelier glass and plasterwork, in the Hotel Continental. A salon of some kind. It was an hour since they had reached the Hotel. A salon, if the gaping walls and broken-up floors and stairwells and roofs open to wind and rain and the night could be called anything such any more. They had entered the hotel through what might once have been its front. It had still been dark, and they were hopeful now but cautious still. They had moved amongst the debris of armchairs, tables and cabinets and Persian carpets scarred and burned. They had split into two groups. He went left, with two others, into the salon where an upright piano stood intact, and so they were not killed instantly when the mortar whooshed in through the wide open hotel frontage. Inside the salon, they fell to the floor. After the explosion they heard Kiwi voices shouting, but across the street, not in the hotel. In the hotel, from the floor above them, they heard returning machine gun fire and German voices yelling back. He waited moments, perhaps minutes, before he crawled belly-down back to the reception area. He saw the officer, sitting, half-toppling, one leg crumpled beneath him but his eyes still open. The other two with the officer, their names not known to him, were not disfigured or bleeding. They lay entwined and dusted with white power from the plaster of ornate cornices, quite dead from the blast. He took their tags without looking at them, put them in his blouse pocket and closed up the metal button. Friendly fire. He took their rifles and some grenades and ammo, and he scuttled back, as low as he could be, to the two men he'd left in the salon. He knew them by name: Nipper and Lofty. He told them to fetch the officer and to carry him between them into the salon. They called the officer Lah-di-dah and were sullen. Then he ordered them to do it. Whatever weapon fire was to be heard was distant now, and the mortars were dropping their shells away from the town.

"Here you are, Taff, the Wounded Hero", Nipper had said, and he and Lofty had slumped Lieutenant Cleave into a heap against the back of an upturned ottoman, as he'd directed them to do. He'd cut up a damask tablecloth to make strips and tied a makeshift tourniquet tightly above the shattered knee. The lower leg was a jagged mess of splintered bone and shredded flesh. Lofty said that young Lah-di-dah had fuckin' had it, the tosser.

He told them to shut it. He positioned Nipper at the entrance to the salon behind the door which hung loose on one hinge. At the far end a hole the size of a window had been made by bomb damage. It looked into a passage between them and other rooms. With Lofty he pulled the piano over to it and they blocked it as much as they could. He told Lofty to sleep and relieve Nipper in an hour. He draped a thick velvet curtain over the officer and sat next to him to wait for the dawn to rise. They would need, he knew, to get out of this trap.

On the floor were scattered pages of musical scores, headed writing paper and envelopes, and picture postcards to send home, of the town, of the abbey. He picked up a couple that were not damaged and pocketed them. The officer touched his arm, softly, almost as a plea. He leaned in to cradle him, holding the young man's slightness in his stockier forearms. It was then he had lit the cigarette and put it between the officer's lips, though he could scarcely draw on it; so he had taken it away and held it himself. The officer drifted in and out of his reverie. So he learned his name and the name of his Cambridge college. Lieutenant Cleave shivered, shook in spasms. He asked to be held closer. Nipper looked over and said Lah-di-dah was fuckin' finished, fuckin' glory hunter, and serve him fuckin' right.

He didn't think Cleave could hear. He hadn't been under this officer's command when the battle had started. Most of those he'd entered the town with were dead, or missing, there or on Castle Hill. He'd known Lofty and Nipper since they'd landed a year before in Sicily. He had nothing good in his heart for them and saw no vantage in friendships so had made none.

Lieutenant Cleave was looking at him in the half-light now filtering into the salon from outside. He was asked for his own name. He gave it. What had he done before the war? He told the officer. His arm was gripped. He was asked if he was a communist. He said no, and the officer giggled and said in Cambridge all miners from South Wales were thought to be communists, or should be, shouldn't they? He said he knew some, but didn't know. He knew miners who were not though. Lieutenant Cleave said that in Cambridge the Party was strong. That he had considered joining, that it was the future, wasn't it? He said he didn't know. The officer asked him what he would do after the war. The pits again? He had no answer to give to that, only felt a need to comfort this boy. He told him, then, that he liked to draw, to sketch, to use pen and ink – some coloured – on scraps of paper or in a notebook he kept of the places he'd seen, or where, to his inner eye, he'd been, even if not as they were. He said he'd show them to him, if he'd like, when it grew light, to see whether he'd actually caught anything right. He meant, though did not say, the whisper of silver among grey-green olive trees in a breeze; the dun colour of crumbling masonry in the southern sun; shadows flitting down the canyons of narrow Neapolitan streets as women strung washing out across the gap between buildings; and the filthy detritus of metal and machines, the scour of a war's passing through all this landscape. The officer said it was a talent, he was sure, and there would, surely, come a time and place for it. No one had said anything like that to him before.

Lieutenant Cleave pulled on the cigarette placed again between his lips. He seemed calmer now, and said that he wished to live, get this bloody leg fixed. In turn, he said nothing of the leg that was, in no real sense, there anymore. But, said the officer, if, you know, things did not work out, then he had a letter on him, half-written before they'd jumped off, and could he send it to Robin, a Cambridge friend, a don in fact, still in college. He said he didn't know what a don was, and Lieutenant Cleave didn't say, only to be sure to include the map he'd made to go with the letter, and that Robin would be so amused by it. It was a map, he said, of this hell they found themselves in.

It was a map Lieutenant Cleave had drawn of the place before its recent full destruction. He said Robin had been his tutor in Classics. Did he, Corporal Maddox, know that the abbey they were fighting to take, the monastery they had flattened into a ruin the previous month, was a sixth-century Benedictine foundation? Despite looting and sieges over centuries it had been a bridgehead, a moral and intellectual powerhouse, between the values of the classical world and the ruins of the barbaric one that had come after it. Robin had wept when the bombs fell unceasingly upon it in February. Robin had written of the new barbarism. Lieutenant Cleave had made the map to show his mentor, graphically, what the world as it was had made of the world of serenity and scholarship now entombed in the monastery on Monte Cassino. It was, he had written, as if a sheet of tracing paper, with place names, real and assigned, had been fitted onto the three-dimensional shapes of the space and collapsed them with the breathtaking mercilessness of time.

"Look, Robin," the letter said of the map, "here is the boundary marker, the river Rapido where the Yanks, attempting to cross by night, were shot up like fish in a barrel in the swollen water at the first battle for Cassino in December. Here, to the north, is the road improbably called Caruso. Did he stay? On his way north, too? In one of the hotels, the one called Roses, or the grander Continental, perhaps? The abbey on the top, squat and all-seeing, window embrasures implacable, shell blasts pocking its walls, its gathered treasures and marbled splendours spirited away along with its monks. Castle Hill, a half-way house, a wind-bitten bastion against ancient quarrels. All around, above and below, ridges, ravines, slopes and flanks of limestone and granite from which troops could almost throw stones at each other, so close are they amongst thickets of brush, thorn and scrub and barbed wire, scarcely dug in; so flinty is the soil, so unyielding the rocks they pick up and pile together to make inadequate defences. *Only not stones, not stones to hurl like children; but grenades, stick bombs, the tracery of automatic fire, the whine of* Nebelwerfers, *the hiss of mortars, the crump of shells. The men look up and call that defile Snakeshead Ridge. They see through the mists the trail of Phantom Ridge and the overhang of cliff just underneath the abbey where a broken pylon sticks out like the shape of a gibbet. So they call that spot Hangman's Hill, with more accuracy than irony."* The lieutenant wondered if Robin thought the names made it all sound rather like an adventure story. *Something like* Swallows and Amazons, *maybe? Or a tale by Robert Louis Stevenson? A dangerous quest for the munificence of the Abbey? A sequel to* Treasure Island? *Lieutenant Cleave asked him if he'd ever read that. It had a map, too, he said. Then the officer closed his eyes again. It was barely dawn. Firing had started again. Nearer this time. He decided they would take the officer with them, and he told Nipper and Lofty they would need to carry him again. He instructed them at the point of a rifle. They cursed, but they lifted the boy, awkwardly because of their respective heights, and slung his arms onto their shoulders. From the back of the hotel, beyond the hole in the wall blocked by the piano, he could hear the turned-over engine of a tank. A Panther. Readying in some part of the building. To the front, through the rubble of the reception area, he glimpsed squads of New-Zealanders, Maori troops, pulling out of the post office, covering each other with fire to break up the machine gun and sniper fire to their left and from on high.*

There were – straight across the mangled jumble of brick and steel and concrete that had been the heart of Cassino – about fifty yards to join up with the Kiwis. They would have to break cover and run and hope to avoid more friendly fire as much as any enemy bullets. He told Nipper and Lofty to shoulder their rifles and run with the officer held between them the moment he opened up with his rifle, aiming high and sightlessly to his right. When they were over where the square had once been, they were to stop in the lee of the post office ruin and shoot as he had done, non-stop to their left, whilst he, in turn, broke cover. He began to fire indiscriminately, and was surprised that the Germans hesitated before returning fire into the hotel they knew was theirs.

More than halfway across, while they were scrambling and trawling the boy along with them, Nipper screamed and fell. Lofty dropped the officer and grabbed at Nipper. He pulled his friend with him, the smaller man's leg grazed by a sniper's shot, half-lifted him and dragged him until they reached – together – a standing pine-end wall, and collapsed – together – behind it. It was then that Lofty shouted back that Lah-di-dah had copped it and that it was every man for his fuckin' self now, Taff, and so long.

* * * * *

When he opened his eyes and shielded them with his coupled hands against the blinding glare of the sun, it was to see Nipper kicking at the upturned soles of his own bootless feet. All around soldiers were out cold or staggering about, their eyes as flat and as empty as of those with battle fatigue, and they had all been to that place without horizons; but this time just because dead-drunk, and still standing. Quick, Taffy, quick, Nipper was saying, pulling at his arm. He sat up and shrugged him off. Nipper was screaming: You gotta help, Taffy, the other buggers are too pissed. He was pointing wildly at the middle vat of fermenting alcohol. Lofty's fallen in, Taff, he said. He's sinking, or something, he said. He's drunk, he said. He said he'd climbed the ladder and that Lofty was gasping, choking, the silly bugger, fell in, didn't he, or something and listen Taff, you cunt, we gotta pull him out. Nipper stopped. I can't swim, you Welsh bastard. I can't swim, Nipper said. I can't do it myself, he said. I've fuckin' tried. Lofty needs help, he said, and these useless twats are no use to anybody, arseholed they are, he said. So come, Taff, quick he said, be a pal, Taffy. He stared at Nipper and he lay back down. He closed his eyes on all the ruins of his life for what he half- hoped might be one last time. He saw again the boy face down in a rain-filled puddle in the small crater of the rubble strewn street where Lofty had dropped him. Nipper was saying, quietly now: Please Taff, please, he'll fuckin' drown otherwise, won't he?

"I fucking hope so, Nipper," he said. "I fucking hope so."

AND AFTER THE WAR, WHAT HAVE
WE LOST? HAVE WE GAINED
ANYTHING? DID YOU?

Oh, I gained all right. Everything. And we all lost, didn't we? For me, though, it was a balance sheet on which my biggest gain was wiped out. You know that. Billy will have told you. You will have seen it. I could feel your sense of my loss. I said nothing, you were too young for that; and besides, I was a kind of curiosity to you, wasn't I? And if I'd said, to either of you, that it wasn't only about Mona not being there, you'd have thought it cold in me, or worse. It wasn't. It isn't. It's what Mona did to me as much as for me that, almost in spite of myself, has made me live on within my despair. She'd made me feel for things: what people did, who they were, why anything mattered. Not just seeing things happen just because they did. That life passed and I could do no more than acknowledge it. The way it had been for me, and nothing more than that since I was a kid.

After I met Mona, though slowly, I'll grant you, my life supports of anger and oblivion weren't enough anymore. I think I resented her for making me face that. I hadn't wanted a future life, just to stretch out the present one as far it'd go without snapping. She made me uncertain, think of letting go, risk letting how we lived now shape the past that was already upon us. Mona didn't teach any of this to me. She spelled nothing out for me. It was the way she lived. I would now call it love, but not as a sentiment. It was more than a single thing. And the love, the sentiment I soon felt for her, was lessened by the real gift she gave me, the one she left me to live with and suffer from. It was to love more than her, or us: to want to reach further than any of us on our own can ever do. Mostly I have failed. Perhaps, as I once thought, the failure has been widespread. Nye Bevan, just before he died, told a close friend that history had given us, that particular working class, our chance, and that we hadn't taken it. I'm no longer so sure of that, of either end of it. What I do know is that the gift cannot be returned. If you take it, you keep it.

The other thing to say is that in those first years after the war it had, for some of the time in some places for some people, all come together. That, I think, is what Bevan meant. The moment. The chance. What had become possible. Of course, some of that feeling, as a supposition, is retrospective, whether as romanticised or evidenced or both. But not completely so. We were teetering on a brink of who we were and might yet be. I was one of those who didn't know this. Not straightaway. And knowledge too often and too readily follows the event, unless it manages to usher in power. That was the debate those who really did know, like Bevan, were trying to lead and influence.

Me, I had just drifted back. Homing pigeon instincts, perhaps, or more like good money calling out to experienced colliers, with the actual work no fright for me and no better prospects before me. I worked in deeper and more mechanised pits, and when I was not slogging at the coal I was sleeping or getting pissed. The pubs were crammed afternoon and night with men crowding up to the bar, no comfort to be had, squabbling over emptied pints since glass was a scarce commodity and someone might nick unseen the one you wanted to fill up again with smelly, local beer, weak as the proverbial piss, of which you'd need a gallon to sink you back to sleep so that you could go again. And again.

It took me nearly three years to get clear of all that; to finally let what had been go. I was bored with being like that, and with myself as well. Life under socialism, in the pits under nationalisation after 1947, was not, in the day-to-day living of it, much different than it had been before the war. You'll read that in some ways it was worse: the rationing, the putting up with shortages, the cold of the coldest winters of the century, the drabness. But, you know, that was only at a remove for us, where we were and how we lived. With work and steady wages we were – together, mind – already in a better place. And if you were there, you could, as well and strange as it might sound, put your finger on a bloody-mindedness which we'd brought back from the war. People knew they'd won something more than a war. It wasn't just who was in power, believe me. It didn't last, I know, and that's my other point – but for a while it was a real, almost tangible thing. It penetrated. It led me to meet Mona.

I was put to work on a heading underground, with her uncle, an older chap and lifelong bachelor. He was the Lodge Sec. as well. Always badgering me about the Fed – the NUM as we were from 1946, membership compulsory now – and politics, of course, though I had cloth ears for all that. But he never stopped going on at me. Finding a way to get to me. Then, once, when we had a spell for snap, he said he'd seen me with a notebook, sketching, he said, so I told him I liked to draw and showed him a few things. He said I should go to an art class, run locally by the WEA: Workers' Educational Association, he said, as if I'd ever heard of it. He said I'd get to use oil paints, on canvas, learn techniques. Well, I never did; not there, though I did pitch up a few times. It was all art history, really, a bit po-faced and respectful, a university type; nice enough; but a bit wet. Still, he pointed me in the way of what they called a settlement, a bus ride away, and there I was let loose to paint and draw and look. Later there were other classes, and then art college. That came after I met Mona, but, see, it was not politics that took me to her, it was the way Isaac Prothero had dressed it up for me and it readied me for change.

Look, there was no conversion or anything. My outlook was being jumbled up, is all. I'm not sure I was exactly happy about it. I stayed surly. From the off she treated me as if I was busted, broken. It was more that I was still indifferent to anything beyond the immediate – what passed for appetite. I saw her like that. And she let me, but only because she saw I knew no different. It took time. Once, early on in our marriage, she cried. I made her cry. I was so angry about her tears. I hadn't understood how they had come. I told her she was soft, being daft; that it was a pointless weeping, that she should grow up and know better. She looked up at me, brushing at the wetness on her face, and it was in a kind of despair at the way this was, and as if I was to be both pitied and hated. I said it was pathetic and that I despised sentimentality. That it was a weakness. The incident was a small one, but it was not petty, and I have never stopped regretting how I was with her that day.

I'd come home from an afternoon shift, washed clean in the new pithead baths. Bone-tired, but wanting to be with her, together alone as we were then. Mona would have been home from the primary school where she taught an hour or so before me. I found her at the table in our back kitchen. There was an old shoe box on the table. She was bent over it. Mona was fussing over a small bird she'd placed in the box, trying to coax it to dip its beak into a saucer of milk. The wren kept toppling from side to side in the box. It made gaspy, choking sounds. She said she'd found it, hopping and falling, in the back yard. That it was distressed. She'd picked it up, cradled it in her hands, and brought it inside. "Look," she'd said, "it's got some wire or something stuck in its beak." I looked, irritated by the care lavished on this hopeless bird. I picked it up. The wire it had swallowed was some unravelled copper cable. It would not tug out. I said the bird would die like this, so better to see it dead soon. That cosseting it was a waste of time. Mona began to cry. I talked harshly, and said things not to be said to those who can love. I was not capable of love like Mona was. I had not yet come to know how to find myself by losing myself in another. By the time I lost her I can say that I had come to know that, and what it was that I was losing. As I say, Bran, there is more to it than this, and for all of us; but it starts from within us or it does not start at all. This cannot be told. It can only be known.

****

He got up from his armchair. He screwed the questionnaire into a ball and let it fall from his hand to the floor. He moved slowly, almost daydreaming, but knowing that he'd decided not to answer, not to tell her. Instead he would reveal to her what he had once tried to do to make some sense, find some light, from the shade of all his remembering. He could never stop remembering. His response to its chaos was graphic. It was to make a mark. A mark that was not of life as such, but a mark made on life itself, a still counterpoint to the restlessness of memory. The paintings he had made after her death were, in colour and in form, antidotes against her being lost to him. Their very abstraction was a riposte, a chiding of the trickery of his having to live on at all. But only Mona had ever been shown the other, this earlier work, and when she died he had gathered them up, put them between tissue paper, and snapped the lock of the suitcase shut on them.

Now, upstairs in the small, cold back bedroom he had used as a studio, he pulled the suitcase down from the top of a single wardrobe – utility furniture from the post-war years – and placed it on a wickerwork chair. He scarcely noticed the flat ribbons of cobweb that twirled from its handle and the fine grain of dust that covered the unopened case. At his feet were the crusted droppings of the acrylic paint he'd used for the abstract canvases. Oil paints spattered the boards of the carpet-less floor. He never looked at the paintings once they were finished. He had stacked them face-in against a wall. In knowing they were finished he also knew that their expression was, for him, limited to the act of doing them. No memories. No traces. No echoes.

He snapped open the catch of the unlocked case. He could not remember whether he had once intended to layer the contents in any order. Yet at the top were the three blank postcards he'd pocketed from the wreckage of the Hotel Continental. Views of Cassino never to be sent, of buildings he'd never seen. The one of the monastery looked almost benign, a benediction on the pre-war town and its people; not the malevolent brooding presence over the valley and their wartime lives which its destroyers had felt as a personalised thing, a warren of spiteful death even after it was reduced to a ruinous heap. The other two postcards were of a lively town, a junction for road and rail halfway between Naples and Rome, a place for travellers and merchants to stop and stay. He remembered how outside that town, on the days before they went into it for the third battle of Cassino, they had been made, officers and NCOs, to study maps in order to memorise the roads, streets and buildings which were meant to guide them to their objectives after the bombing by air and the shelling by artillery had stopped. Strategic points to capture, to hold, to reinforce for attack on the stone husk that the monastery already was. The post office. The railway station. Hotels. Castle Hill. The bends and plateaux up the hills to the prize itself: the monastery. In one postcard he could clearly see the open piazza, its trees for shade, the hotel windows shuttered against the sun, the road climbing away up to the knoll of Castle Hill. But when they crept into Cassino behind the tanks that spluttered and stalled, none of these former things were left to be seen. Whatever had been the sign of human settlement had been erased, made to vanish along with the people long fled to caves and the mountains, all who had once lived there. The postcards held between his fingers were curled at their edges, and the place they had pictured for that moment had, he knew, been rebuilt. If so, it was apparently the same, even down to the monastery; recreated stone by stone and its manuscript treasures all returned, even the graves of all who had died there become an encircling diadem of further homage. He had seen those post-war magazine pictures, too. Another world created to make new the old one which had gone. He felt no grudge for this, only that it was not, either old or new, the world that was the end of the world, which was what he knew when he had been there.

Beneath the postcards there was a sheaf of drawings. Black-and-white like the postcards, but with nothing poignant with charm in their subject matter. Scrolls of coiled barbed wire and fenced-in munition dumps and the prowling about on the heaped ruins of feral tanks. He remembered how, with no sense of unease amidst the collapse of all civilised certitude at Cassino, he had gleefully sat to one side working on paper in pen and ink as the troops swept across the finally bridged river through the town's rubbled remains into the expanse of the Liri Valley, onto fabled Route Six to Rome and another ending. He picked out the one he would show her to make his particular confession of barbarianism.

He remembered the moment and its setting. Here were the charred stumps of the fire blackened trees which had, in the pre-war postcards, once titillated Cassino with their fritillary of palm fronds and tracery of leaves. Their gracefully scalloped trunks had been twisted into grotesqueries of shape, leafless lumps of charcoal, and what had been the waving branches of trees were skeletal limbs, snapped and torn into supplicant form. By the marks he had made on paper the eye was drawn up a makeshift road to the shell-blasted hill with its crumbling tower. In the drawing the way up to the battered walls of the redoubt on Castle Hill was not a smoothly inviting transit as it was in the postcard, nor a morass of stone and brick and hillocks of torn metal as when soldiers had picked their way over its murderous passage. He revealed it as it had become after the final battle in May 1944 had been won: just a bulldozed and cleared pathway on whose winding way an armoured car bounced along.

He held the drawing, and looked at it with a misery which was almost fear at the thought of the thing he was then. The horror he had depicted had been done, he knew, with the energy of exultation. The vehicle in his picture careered skittishly around the water-filled voids where the bombs and shells had struck again and again. It raced where they had once fought in a crawl, night and day, to the hill above the road. The armoured car in his picture, was jaunty in its motion and, as he'd sat there at the roadside and watched it jounce past, he had cheered and loved its fuck-you joy-ride through the precincts of what had been hell. He knew in the years that came on and changed him that the gladness he had felt then in the very pit of his stomach was an emotion available to him because he had once been other. Other than human, even. He was not sure whether this carapaced otherness only came to him because of the war, but he knew that what the war had done to him was a terrible completion. It was not, either, that he had lived and those others had not. That species of fear and the instinctive grab at survival had long left him. The dread he shivered at again, in this cold, upstairs back bedroom decades after the war had ended, was the dread of being at one with destruction. The ease of it; the exquisite pleasure in being a part of all the destruction. His sketch was a barbaric yell against all that was said to have been better about places like Monte Cassino. That was the horror.

* * * * *

He sat, disconsolate, on the shabby pink candlewick counterpane of the room's single bed. He spread out the works, drawings and paintings, which had once unlocked the closure of past memory. He knew what had been unlocked had given him a different space to locate himself in between the harsh lines of his early drawings and the depthless abstraction that would come later. It was how the horror had been faced down. This is what he needed Bran, or someone, to know – and that it was key. He decided to try to explain that the scorn they all felt from his tongue during the last strike was not from anger, but from love. This was the bullion of his values, he wanted to say, not some kind of promissory political note to cash in via a Utopian treasury of ideology. That he had been shown how to live. That this could extend beyond the personal, but in any case existed even if it failed to do so. Not activism. Not even consciousness. Not enough so, anyway. That what he had once learned was, for him, the only true justification of that final strike's ultimate thrashing about in a death throe of common dismay. That it was a convulsion of rebellion. A testament of love for some ways of living that had once been glimpsed and sometimes enacted. And that he knew it was being betrayed, that dream of reality, by themselves as they role-played it into oblivion.

He would need to tell her about Mona. He did not know how he could. He had failed to tell his own son. If he tried it all came in cameos of truthfulness that were also meaningless. She had, as everyone said who knew them then in the immediate years after the war, saved him. From what? From himself, they'd say. He had drifted back, almost despite himself, to the coalfield. A different valley. A different town. Fierce drinking in the dozens of pubs that winked at you over such a few miles, walking from lodgings to the pit to the town and its villages, to a dance, to a meeting hall. He went through the alphabet to recall them all from A to Z, from the Albion Hotel to the Zetetics Tavern, where they drank bitter and whiskey on the weekend – men only except for the jug-and-bottle siderooms for women fetching and quaffing milk stout, the colliers standing at the bar in battledress and berets, safety helmets scorned underground by these men, coal dirt and grime scrubbed off – and into affiliated clubs on Sundays when the pubs were shut, girls fed port-and-lemon in the lounge bars and taken outside, later, into back lane *gwlis* or abandoned mountainside quarries.

More pubs than chapels. More drinkers than believers. More standing room for boozers than pews for worshippers. He had sunk into his own oblivion, and relished it. He would never have met Mona nor have wanted to meet anyone like her, until, that is, he did. Bran would assume he meant passion or sex or perhaps love, but it was not any of those things, at least not in themselves. It was instead the possibility he saw that he would no longer need to be alive for himself alone. It was, Mona had said, his vulnerability, not his strength, which had drawn her to him. The strength, she'd said, was all-too-bloody obvious and came out in him as unflinching, sullen and isolate. There was, she said, no connective tissue, as if all his nerve-ends had been burned out. She set out to reignite him.

He was thirty-three when they met in 1948. She was ten years younger, a trained primary school teacher and the niece of a fellow coal-face worker, a bachelor who'd casually invited him, after a Sunday lunchtime session in the Albion, to his younger sister's home for "a cooked dinner". Mona had been there, small and pert, her hair dark and short, her tongue quick and vivid. Her parents, William and Maggie Roberts, miner and housewife, were lively talkers, too, and active in the Communist Party branch. Neither he later nor Mona then ever joined the Party as such, less out of negative conviction but more out of an acceptance that fell short of a formal political allegiance; but both were absorbed by its wider culture. He remembered the issues, the debates, the quarrels, that turn-of-the-tide which they first expected and then anticipated flowing on into the next decade, even long after it had ebbed away. Looking back, the detail of intent was still sharply defined. Then, all blurred and stalled. An empty echo, because there was no conceivable effectiveness to conjure up anymore. What had been ensured for him, though, was the desire he had found to fulfill himself. But only for her, so that the physical bond could become, beyond inevitable change, an unbreakable emotion.

For Bran to begin to grasp what he had gained and what was lost in the years after the war, she would need to feel how the limitations of his world and of himself became distant horizons to be reached, not personalised boundaries to be broached. This was what love with Mona had become. And when they made love or sated all the impossible, ravenous hunger which makes lovers, for a time anyway, immortal and the actual business of living immaterial, then they embodied the future they would, so unexpectedly, share.

What others would depict as the dull monotony of the fifties, a conformist decade sandwiched between the upheaval of the forties and the release of the sixties, he had felt as fulfillment. For him and, he suspected, others of his kind – and generationally there were many – domesticity was revolutionary. What might be seen as routine, for men as much as for women, was revelatory: the world could, in instances, be put on hold. Between the bedlam of war and the narcissism of plentifulness they nestled, safe and quiet, from all discontents. If he thought, carefully, back to what had been lost, it was this momentary stasis which haunted him most. And if he could no longer, with any certainty of sensation, taste the soft and cool freshness of her skin or scent the delicate air which surrounded her, he could still see the spiral of green apple skin which she could pare expertly away from the flesh of the fruit they would share, and could look again in memory at the curl and tuft of her hair as it bunched at the nape of a neck he could still see himself, awake more than in any dream, bending down to kiss. His few years with Mona were brief, but their very brevity weighted them, one by one and moment by moment, with an intensity that bore down on him. He made a dry-point etching for each year they had had together. Always a fern, or rather the imprint of a fern. A fossil preserved inside a lump of shining coal and crushed beneath the earth for eons of time. Crack open the coal lump and there it was, each frond and tendril as it once was and will always now be. He made the imprint into an ethereal, ghostly tracing, a defiant whisper of what was a presence yet, despite all time. Even so it was only a hint of what he knew he had been once promised, shown and given, as an exit from the ruins.

The year before he married Mona, eight years after Cassino, one year before the gadarene goggling at the Coronation, six years before she would die haemorrhaging unstoppably while giving birth to Billy, he had made a small oil painting on board. His work in those years, after the pit and into the adult education classes that had led to art school, was mostly in watercolour and mostly landscapes, swirling and swoony arabesques of road and hill and buildings. It was a different kind of mapping of the places he knew. He ingested their undeniable shapes, often grotesque and unwieldy as places for people to inhabit, and, with what he had come to know, he digested their meaning as to how they had shaped a latent aspiration. He believed in this, and he believed in the wider values which love had, at last, caused him to embrace. The oil painting, though, was different again. He had not intended it for storytelling, but when it was done, he had seen immediately how numinous it was in its placing of people within its frame.

The summation was in the title he had given to the work. It was just a name – yet it was, he knew in 1952, a name as closed off and threatening as it was beckoning and seductive. The name was "Glamorgan", and the painting was, in its effect at least, a bridge. From its depths it led the eye out of the expressed connotations of that name, its very history, and through and up into an imaginary sense of its being. Wherever you looked, the literal properties of that past sprung up from the shadowplay of its painterly evoking. And the deeper and wider you looked into the picture, the more three-dimensional and solid were its church spires and its chapel frontages, and the more rounded and perpendicularly thrusting were its chimneys, the more substantial the terraced housing and artisan villas. All that world of work and ownership and settlement and riches and faith was signalled to the eye by the smoke of its industry and by the smudge of black tip waste on the bumped out curves of the squat hills. In the centre of the frame there was an excavation, inexplicable in any bland reality; a void in which the houses on its rim above were inverted so that they floated as if in a shimmering expanse of water. Outlying lucent greens and tawny ochres yielded to blues and violet hues and the pinks of a dropping dusk. A road climbed, winding and steep, from the clustered townships, wending up and around and across the picture. At the road's summit, walls and façades were falsities, one brick thick, with glassless windows blown out. An older man, a father perhaps, stood to one side beneath a lamppost that gave no light. A woman, a mother once perhaps, peered out from behind a wall and, in stiff repose, made no gesture of embrace from the fate of her entrapment. Only two lovers, caught between all else but animated, together, seemed to promise still to follow the road out, escaping walls and ruins and the cruciform pole and crossbars of the gas lamp standing sentinel over the slaughterhouse that had been his Glamorgan.

When he had finished looking back and inwards, he put everything back into the suitcase and carried it downstairs to the warmth and light of his knock-through living room. He sat, perfectly still, in his armchair. He closed his eyes and, with ease, he slept.

* * * * *

When he did not answer to her light knock, Bran tried the knob of the unlocked door and let herself in. He was still asleep. On the table in the centre of the room she saw her recorder. She picked it up. She saw that the tape had wound to an end. She switched the tape-recorder's button to "off" and put the machine in a pocket of her jacket. She placed a bottle of Irish whiskey – Bushmills, his favourite – in the centre of the table. She walked towards him, seeing the small suitcase upright at his feet. She reached down to shake his shoulders, and gave them a gentle push. He stirred and half-opened his eyes. "I let myself in", she said, as if he required an explanation for her being there. She tapped, with one finger, the tape recorder in her pocket. She said, "I want to thank you. Very much, Dai. For this. And for what you've been able to tell me. Thank you." He appeared startled, dazed from the sleep. She smiled at him and said, bending down to pick up her crumpled questionnaire from the carpet, "And for following instructions, eh?" Bran laughed when she said this bent over and kissed him on his forehead.

"Look, Bran", he said, and leaned forward in his chair as she stood up in front of him, "Look, I don't think I can help you." She said he wasn't to be daft. He said that the thing was he was sure he couldn't say what she wanted – needed – him to say. She shook her head at his foolishness. Her bunched hair swayed around her neck, glinting as blue as it was black as it was caught in the last light of the day. But, he said, she was to have the suitcase – this case, he said – and, if she liked, she could look at the things in it, ask him other questions perhaps, or give it to Billy if he ever came back and if he, himself, had gone. He told her, and he could not hide the catch in his voice, that it was from Mona, for them both, as well as from him. Tired, more than he had felt for a long time, exhausted by effort, he wiped a hand across his eyes. He blinked with their wetness.

"You're a lovely old bugger, you know," Bran told him. "Please, Dai, don't cry. Not now." She kneeled before him and held his head between her hands. She stroked his cheek. She put her two hands behind his head and pulled it downwards, towards her. She said, "This is for Billy, eh?", and moved her face closer and kissed him on his lips, and he raised his head slowly, as if in a dream.

* * * * *

In her car, driving back down and out of the valley to the city, she hoped he would have no regrets. He deserved it, she thought. Both him and Billy. In both senses. She had placed the tape recorder on the passenger seat and had pressed the rewind button before she'd set off so that she could listen to the tape as she drove. Now, she pressed the "Play" button, and the sound was of silence, other than the working noise of the machine itself, just a wordless silence. She rewound and pressed "Play" again. Except for the sound of the spools which whirred and whirred beside her, there was only his silence.